**W9-COB-905**

halfway to the SKY

to the

ALSO BY KIMBERLY BRUBAKER BRADLEY

Ruthie's Gift
One-of-a-Kind Mallie
Weaver's Daughter

halfway to the SKY
to the

Kimberly Brubaker Bradley

DELACORTE PRESS

Published by
Delacorte Press
an imprint of
Random House Children's Books
a division of Random House, Inc.
1540 Broadway
New York, New York 10036

Visit us on the Web! www.randomhouse.com/kids
Educators and librarians, for a variety of teaching tools, visit us at
www.randomhouse.com/teachers

Library of Congress Cataloging-in-Publication Data

Bradley, Kimberly Brubaker.
  Halfway to the sky / Kimberly Brubaker Bradley.
     p. cm.
  Summary: After her brother dies and her parents get a divorce, twelve-year-old
Katahdin sets out to hike the whole Appalachian Trail from Georgia to Maine on her own.
   ISBN 0-385-90029-5 (lib. bdg.) — ISBN 0-385-72960-X
   [1. Hiking—Fiction. 2. Appalachian Trail—Fiction. 3. Mothers and daughters—
Fiction. 4. Grief—Fiction. 5. Divorce—Fiction.] I. Title.
   PZ7.B7247 Hal 2002
   [Fic]—dc21

                                                          2001037246

The text of this book is set in 11.5-point Times New Roman.
Book design by Melissa J Knight
Map by Virginia Norey

Manufactured in the United States of America
April 2002
10 9 8 7 6 5 4 3 2 1
BVG

To Bart

for the hiking boots for Christmas

the trek up Springer Mountain

the freezing Fourth of July night
in the shelter on Mount Greylock

the week at muscular dystrophy camp

and mostly

for your unwavering belief in me
and for the life we share

Thank you

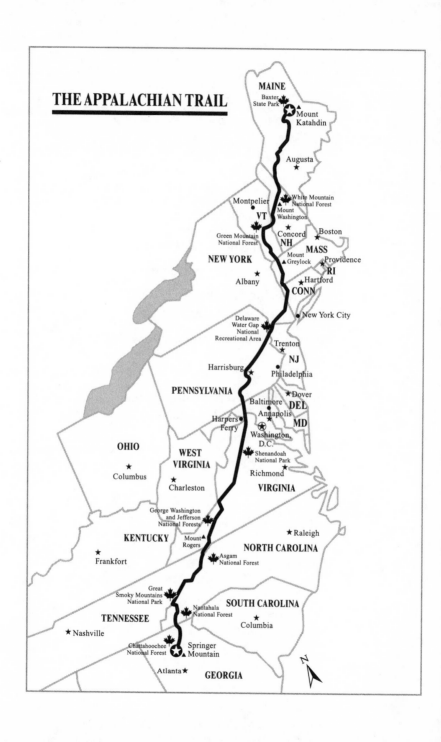

THE APPALACHIAN TRAIL

Remote for detachment,

narrow for chosen company,

winding for leisure,

lonely for contemplation,

the Trail leads not merely north and south

but upward to the body, mind and soul of man.

—Harold Allen

March 1
3326 Holston Drive, Bristol, Tennessee
Miles hiked today: 0 (so far)
Total miles hiked on the Appalachian Trail: 0
Weather: bright, mid-50s, very windy

I went through my pack one more time.

Sleeping bag, pad, tent, stove. Fuel, food bag, toothbrush, towel. Extra shorts, shirt, tights, fleece jacket, one each. Extra socks, sock liners, underwear, two pairs each. Dr. Bronner's peppermint soap. Maps for the first leg. One small notebook, a few handwritten lists, and a photograph of Springer.

I tightened the drawstring and lifted the pack carefully onto my shoulders, then fastened it around my hips and across my chest. Fully loaded, the pack weighed 33 pounds on the bathroom scale. Fully dressed, I weighed 115. That was counting my boots, which were nearly a pound apiece.

It was a Wednesday. I should have been in school. I looked around my room. Pink walls—we painted them when I was seven. Flowered bedspread, the bed neatly made. My soccer ball, the only thing I wished I could take but couldn't, and the trophies and the posters and the dolls. Everything painfully neat, dusted, wiped clean. I looked around and thought, *It should not be so easy for a twelve-year-old girl to run away.*

But it was.

I clicked the door shut and went across the darkened hall and down the stairs. Sometimes our house seemed like a museum, full of stuff but not a place where people actually lived. The kitchen was antiseptic. Mom scrubbed when she couldn't sleep at night. Lately that was most of the time.

I paused in the foyer and hit the Record button on the answering machine. I cleared my throat. "Look, Mom, it's me, Dani," I said, in what I hoped was the right sort of voice, half angry, half sulky. I'd picked a fight with her the night before on purpose to give me an excuse to sound like this. As usual, she had left the house before I woke. She worked strange hours these days, and not because she had to, either. Who ever heard of starting at seven in the morning at a bank? "I don't want to live with you anymore, okay?" I said to the machine. Sulk, sulk. "I'm going to Dad's for a while. Maybe forever. So don't call. Bye."

I hit the button again, and the little light started blinking. Messages—1. Two nights before, Dad had told me he couldn't see me this weekend because he was going out of town. So when Mom did get around to calling, he wouldn't be there. I figured I'd have a whole week to get away. I didn't think they'd guess where I'd gone. The Appalachian Trail was a legend in our family, but my parents had quit telling the stories about it long ago.

I went to the front door, opened it, hesitated, went back. Springer's room on the first floor was dark and stale-smelling, the curtains drawn, the hospital bed shrouded with a plain white sheet. Clean vacuuming lines ran up and down the carpet, untouched. No one had stepped inside for weeks. I didn't either. "Hey," I said softly, "I'm leaving now. I'm doing this for you, too. Okay?"

It shouldn't be easy for a thirteen-year-old boy to die. But it was.

I locked the door on my way out.

The Greyhound depot was in the middle of town, a twenty-minute walk away. I had already bought my ticket to Gainesville, Georgia, and no one asked me questions. I'd thought they would. I'd thought someone would wonder why I was alone, why I was carrying such a heavy pack, why I wasn't in school. There were six other passengers at the Bristol stop. None of them paid any attention to me.

In a car it would have taken less than five hours to reach Gainesville, but on the bus it took all day. We stopped, and stopped, and stopped again. Once, I got off to pee in a dingy station, but other than that I stayed put with my pack wedged in the space in front my knees. When I got hungry, I ate some of my raisins. I didn't get thirsty or tired. I looked out the window and tried not to think about anything.

The Appalachian Trail runs 2,167 miles from Georgia to Maine, mostly along the ridgelines of mountains. It's a high-up kind of place. It ends on the top of Mount Katahdin, in Maine, and begins on the top of Springer Mountain, in Georgia. Each year about three thousand people try to hike the whole Trail from beginning to end in a single year. The ones who make it are called thru-hikers.

My parents had been thru-hikers fourteen years earlier. They met for the first time their first night on the Trail. They got married partway through, and by the time they reached Katahdin, Mom was pregnant with my brother. They named him Springer because he was part of the Trail. When I was born a year later, they named me Katahdin, to match, but everyone calls me Dani. When Springer couldn't walk anymore, my parents put their memories of the Trail away.

Dad still hiked. He went away by himself for long days every few months in decent weather. "I need an escape, Dani," he'd tell me. "I need to be alone." He bought me hiking boots and took me for walks in the park near our house. He taught me some things, but not much.

Mom never hiked. She never did anything but go to work, take care of Springer, and run three miles every morning while I made breakfast by myself.

Springer, Springer. I found myself tracing his name on the grimy window with my finger. An old woman sitting across the aisle glared at me. I wiped the window with my sleeve and folded my hands.

There's a trick to not thinking, and I'd learned it.

From Gainesville I took a taxi, the way the guidebooks suggested. The driver tried to talk to me, but I shut my eyes and he left me alone. When I opened them, I saw a strange ugly forest, hills that looked different from the ones we had at home. It was evening, and I was hungry.

"Here we go," the cabbie said. He swung right and stopped. A big wooden sign read AMICALOLA FALLS STATE PARK. "I'm not going through the gates," he said. "Have to pay a park fee if I do. Drop you here, okay, sis?"

"Okay." I paid him, dragged my pack out of the backseat, and watched him drive away. I looked at the park entrance again. I was here. The books all say it takes five million steps to walk the entire Appalachian Trail. I took my first one, breathed deep, and smiled.

March 1
Amicalola Falls State Park Shelter (Georgia)
Miles hiked today: 1
Total miles hiked on the Appalachian Trail: 0
Weather: clear, getting cold

The man at the park gate waved me through without making me pay. I saw that the sign said two dollars per vehicle, and I guessed that since I was walking I didn't count. I wondered if he would remember me, if someone came looking for me, if there was a search team or something. I hoped not. I was wearing a wool hat, and I pulled it farther down so he couldn't see my face.

I walked along the road toward the buildings just ahead. Mountains rose up in a half-circle in front of me. I felt like I was walking into the bottom of a bowl. The sun was almost down, and the trees, still bare of leaves, shone golden brown in the fading orange light. The pine trees closer to me were scraggy and wild.

There were cars in the parking lot, but no people that I could see. The road forked, signs pointing one way to the campground, another to the lodge. The visitors' center was closed, which pleased me; the toilets were locked, which didn't. Behind the building I found a perfect rectangle of lawn, bordered with stone walls and bisected by a sidewalk that led beneath a stone archway to a packed dirt trail.

The start of the approach trail.

I had read all about it. Something as grand and difficult as the Appalachian Trail would never start at the *bottom* of a mountain; it starts at the top, at the very summit of Springer. So the approach trail runs nine miles uphill to that start. The guidebooks all say things like "Don't think the approach trail is any walk in the park," which is pretty stupid given how much of the Trail really is a walk in some kind of park. But I understood that the approach trail was going to be difficult, and looking at the bottom of it, I could see why. It meandered up through the trees, up to the left, and up, up, up. I had read that of the three thousand people trying to thru-hike in any of the more recent years, over ten percent never made it to the top of Springer. Ten percent never made it to the *start*.

Only another ten percent actually made it all the way to Katahdin. But I figured most of them didn't want to get there as badly as I did. Even with the heavy pack holding me back, my legs, my shoulders, my brain all seemed to pull me forward, faster. Away, away.

But not that night. It was getting dark quickly, and the air was cold and damp. I went through the archway and up the hill a few steps, then left—and there, exactly where the books said it would be, was a shelter. Dark and empty, more good luck.

The shelter had a roof and three wooden walls, and a screened-in front with a door. Inside, two rows of bunks with wire mesh bottoms stretched from one side of the shelter to the other. Room for eight, more in a pinch. I peed behind a bush just outside the shelter, then went inside, unrolled my sleeping bag across a bottom bunk in the corner, and unloaded most of my gear. I found my stove, my fuel bottle, my water bottles—all full—my pot and my food bag. I set up the stove on the platform in front of the shelter, just the way I'd practiced at home. I reached into my pack for my matches to light it.

Except that I didn't have matches. My hand closed on the empty film canister I'd meant to fill with matches just as my brain remembered I hadn't done it. I'd had to put most of my gear together at the last minute to keep things secret. We had lots of matches in the kitchen at home. I'd forgotten them.

I dumped everything out of my food bag. Noodles, soup mixes, hot chocolate. Instant oatmeal, tea. I'd chosen food that was light and wouldn't spoil—and therefore, food that needed to be mixed with water and boiled. I was getting colder, and I wanted something hot. The shelter was awfully dark now, too. I didn't have a flashlight because I didn't think I could afford the batteries, and I didn't want to carry anything I couldn't use.

Don't panic, I told myself. I didn't. I ate the rest of my raisins and one of my three chocolate bars, and the apple I'd picked up on my way out of the house that morning. I drank some cold water, stirred more water into a packet of instant oatmeal, and made myself eat it even though it tasted like sweet, gritty glue. I used the water in my second bottle to rinse the bowl and spoon, realized I didn't have any water left to brush my teeth, and decided I'd look for water in the morning. There had to be some somewhere.

By now I was really cold, but I remembered that I was supposed to take some of my clothes off, or else the sweat trapped in them would condense inside my sleeping bag. I took my jacket off and, after some thought, my socks. I put on a clean pair of socks and my second shirt and climbed into my icy sleeping bag. Then I remembered I'd forgotten to hang up my food.

If you don't hang up your food at night, mice eat it, or worse, bears. I jumped out of my sleeping bag, shivering violently, stuffed all the food I could find into my food bag, and after three tries managed to throw a rope around one of the shelter's rafters and hang the bag from the ceiling. I jumped back into my sleeping bag and lay shivering while I wondered what else I'd forgotten.

Matches were easy. I could get matches anywhere. I went through a mental list of everything I'd meant to bring, and tried to picture where each item was inside my pack. I thought I'd remembered everything else.

It was probably only about seven o'clock—I couldn't read my watch in the dark—and I wasn't really sleepy, but I didn't have anything else to do. When I had tried to imagine what life on the Trail would be like, I'd always pictured the shelters crowded with people, happy people, all happy to be hiking the Trail. It had never occurred to me that I'd spend my first night alone. I couldn't see the moon from the inside of the shelter. I wondered if there were stars.

I was used to waking up alone and getting myself off to school, but I'd never been alone at night before. It was an inter- esting feeling. After a while I found I didn't mind it. I wasn't scared, not with the Trail so close and the shelter walls around me. Maybe this was how my parents felt, their first night out, before they found each other, before the disasters began. Maybe they had been happy.

I woke in the night, shivering. My sleeping bag was rated to twenty degrees, but it must have been below that, and I'd been stupid enough to take off my hat. I got up and fumbled in the dark, trying to find it and my fleece jacket. Suddenly I heard a noise almost exactly under my left hand, a rough, low growl that did not sound like a mouse or an insect or anything else I expected in a shelter. I screamed.

The thing on the bunk rolled over with a swish of nylon and sat up partway and became a man, a hiker, sleeping in his own sleeping bag. He looked up. "Problem?" he asked.

I put my hands over my mouth. "I thought you were a bear."

He seemed to consider this for a moment. "The shelters with closed-in fronts, you'd hear a bear trying to get in," he said.

"I didn't hear you come in." I shivered again, found my jacket, and pulled it on.

He laughed. "True. But I'm quieter than your average bear. Better with door handles, too."

I was beginning to feel really dumb, so I climbed back into my bag. "Sorry," I said.

He rolled over in his bag. "No problem. Good night."

March 2
Summit of Springer Mountain (Georgia)
Miles hiked today: 8
Total miles hiked on the Appalachian Trail: 0
Weather: sunny, cold

In the morning the sound of birds chirping woke me. I sat up and looked around. The sky above the bare trees was a bright, clear blue. Next to me, the other hiker's sleeping bag was empty. I could see him standing far off in the woods, very still with his back toward me. I started to shout, then realized that he was peeing. I looked down. I had to pee, too, quite badly in fact, and though I didn't mind the idea of peeing in the woods, doing it in daylight when there were no leaves on the bushes and a man around and who knew who else was somewhat upsetting. Maybe the visitors' center was open. I checked my watch. Seven A.M. Probably not.

The man came in whistling cheerfully. "Morning," he said. "Do I look like a bear in the daylight?"

He had sandy hair and long ears and a thin nose. His eyes were blue and very bright, and the skin around his neck seemed to sag a little even though he was quite thin. He was younger than I would have guessed. Older than Springer, but not by much. "You look like a beagle," I said without thinking.

He laughed. His eyes twinkled and he had very white teeth. "Well, look out," he said. "I hear the Smoky Mountains are just jam-packed full of beagles."

"Look," I said, "if I go out there and, um, admire nature, um, like you just did, would you mind not watching?"

"No problem," he said. "You could go behind the shelter, but it's kind of in view of the parking lot."

I was quick, but by the time I got back he had already rolled his sleeping bag and was ready to leave. It looked like he'd hardly unpacked anything the night before. "So, are you thru-hiking?" he asked.

"Yes," I said.

He grinned, then looked away. "Look. I hate to ask, it's kind of personal and all that—to each his own, you know, or her own—but how old are you?"

"Twelve," I said. "How old are you?"

He grinned. "Seventeen. Okay, so I shouldn't have much to say, right? But do your folks know you're out here?"

"Yes," I said. The shorter the lie, the better.

He didn't look like he believed me. "If I was going to lie to you," I said, "would I have told you I was twelve?"

He shrugged. "Hey, how do I know, right? The thing is, you look twelve. I wouldn't have believed you if you'd said you were seventeen."

I looked him right in the eye. "I wouldn't have believed you if you said you were twelve."

Beagle laughed. "Hike your own hike," I added. That was another phrase from the guidebooks. It meant that everyone came to the Trail for different reasons, and hiked it differently too, some fast, some slow, and so on. It meant other thru-hikers were supposed to respect you, no matter what.

"Okay," Beagle said. "Whatever." He held out his hand. "I'm William Knowlton."

I shook his hand. "Dani Brown."

He said, "You're *thru*-hiking? It's a long way."

I glared at him.

"Yeah, okay, sorry. At least you look like a hiker. Let me give you some advice, Hike-Your-Own-Hike Dani Brown. Don't do the first mile of the approach trail. It's a killer. Not worth it. Hitch a ride to the top of the falls and start from there. And don't bother making yourself breakfast this morning. Up by the falls they've got a lodge, and the breakfast buffet is an All-You-Can-Eat." He grinned. "That's the first rule of thru-hiking: Never pass up an All-You-Can-Eat."

Unless the All-You-Can-Eat costs money, I thought. I'd saved all I could for this trip—birthday presents, Christmas presents, plus I'd baby-sat the neighbor's wretched six-year-old twice a week after school and every single day Christmas break—but I'd had to buy a lot of my equipment, too, and I only had about five hundred dollars to last the trip. The books said to count on six months for a thru-hike, so that worked out to twenty dollars a week for food, as long as none of my gear broke. Not many restaurant meals there. I shook my head. "I haven't tried hitchhiking yet and I'm not hungry."

At that exact moment my stomach growled like it was being torn in two. Beagle laughed. Even I smiled.

"You know you'll end up hitching sometimes?" he said.

I nodded. The books all said so, but I wasn't very happy about doing it. Never trust a stranger, and all that.

"All right, Dani Brown," William said. "Here's what. We'll hitch a ride up together, and I will treat you to your very first All-You-Can-Eat. I'll buy. Deal?"

"You don't have to buy me breakfast."

"You can . . . I don't know what—make me cocoa later on. Okay?"

"Okay," I said. I probably shouldn't have agreed, but I liked Beagle.

"Did your mother teach you not to talk to strangers?" he asked while I packed my gear.

"Yes," I said.

"What about hitching rides and eating breakfast with them?" he asked.

"You're not a stranger," I said.

He didn't smile; in fact, he looked concerned. "I'm not," he said. "And you can trust me; you can trust most people out here. But you ought to be careful, Dani Brown."

I hoisted my pack. "I am," I said. "I always am."

We got a hitch from a man driving a pickup truck, who stopped and motioned us toward the truck bed. Beagle dropped the tailgate and gave me a hand up. The road was so steep it was scary, and I'd never been in the back of a truck before. But the air was crisp and the mountains were beautiful, and Beagle was laughing. I felt like I was starting a fabulous adventure.

The falls were puny, disappointing. "You expected Niagara?" Beagle asked.

"Something," I said.

He shook his head. "You haven't spent much time around here, have you?"

"Sure I have."

"Hike much?"

"Every day for two hours since December."

He nodded. "Thought so. You seem strong."

The lodge looked more like a Holiday Inn than anything I ever expected to see on the top of a mountain. But the breakfast was indeed All-You-Can-Eat. I winced when Beagle paid $6.95 for each of us.

"Don't worry about it," he said.

"Are you rich?" I helped myself to sausages, six of them, and pancakes, and eggs. The smells from the buffet were wonderful. I was starving.

"Nope," he said cheerfully. "But that's okay. Can't have you starting off hungry, can we?"

"Are you in college?" I asked.

We had found a table by the windows and sat down. The restaurant wasn't crowded, though there were a few other people who looked like potential thru-hikers to me.

Beagle drank a full glass of orange juice straight down. "No," he said, wiping his lips. "I graduated from high school in January. I took extra classes for the last two years so I could finish a semester early. I've always wanted to try a thru-hike, and my folks said I could if I did it this way. I start classes at Duke in September."

I didn't know what Duke was but decided not to ask. "That's cool," I said. I bit into my pancakes.

"What about you?" asked Beagle.

Ouch. I should have known better than to ask him questions; it made him feel he could ask me questions in return. "I don't know," I said.

He squinted at me. "Really?"

"Really."

"Your parents just said, whatever, take off from school, disappear for six months, you're on your own?"

"Yeah."

"That sounds like child abuse."

"No—they just . . ." I looked out the window. The view was incredible. I couldn't talk about Springer, not in this restaurant. "They met on the Trail," I said. "The very first night."

Beagle looked at me in a funny way all through the rest of the meal, but he didn't ask me anything else. I was glad.

The trail above the falls was not as steep as the trail below them, but it was steep enough. Beagle strode ahead of me, quickly disappearing from sight. He walked bouncily, like he had springs on his feet. I had hiked every afternoon on the streets around our neighborhood to get ready for this, but I didn't walk the way Beagle did. My pack dug into my shoulders. I trudged.

The trail was a beaten path through the naked woods, but it was neither smooth nor straight. I found myself watching my feet, both to be sure I didn't trip and because my pack tended to tip my head forward. I tripped anyway. Several times.

"So, Dani, what did you see on your historic walk?"

"Mostly the tops of my boots."

"What did you think about while you were walking?"

"Nothing. The less I thought, the better."

I walked carefully, quietly, slowly, I supposed, but steadily. My heart pounded. I didn't see Beagle for what I figured was at least a mile. I didn't see anybody, even though I knew there were other thru-hikers around—at the lodge I'd caught a glimpse of one arranging her pack in the lobby. I didn't see squirrels, birds, anything. The wind blew. The air was cold, but I was wearing my hat and my fleece and my thermal under-wear, and I was warmer than I wanted to be.

Step, step, step. Breathe, breathe, breathe. Step, step. Georgia to Maine. I tried to imagine what it was like for the people who quit right here, who walked the trail I was walking and decided it was too much—they preferred to go home.

In the first place, they probably had a home to go to.

Me, I felt like I could walk forever.

15

I went around a turn and saw Beagle sitting on a log beside the trail eating a handful of something. He saw me and smiled. He'd taken his hat off and hung it from his pack on a cord. "Gorp?" he asked. I shook my head. "Gotta keep eating, sis," he said.

"I've got plenty," I said. I did, too, it was just all in my pack, which I didn't feel like taking off. "Later," I said.

He shrugged. "See you," he said. "Two miles down now. Six to go." He walked off, pulling ahead of me like the pack on his back weighed nothing, like he'd been walking forever and meant to do it about that much more. I felt slow compared to him, but I didn't feel bothered.

Hike your own hike. My hike did not include needing to be supervised or given handouts of gorp. I was out here to be alone. I began to regret accepting breakfast from him, except that the sausages had been so awfully tasty.

I saw Beagle again a few miles on, and again a bit after that. "I don't need a baby-sitter," I told him. "I *am* a baby-sitter. I'm a hiker, too. I'm fine."

"Hey, sis," he said genially, "if you were my sister, I'd be wanting someone to check in with you now and then."

"I'm not your sister." I surprised myself by how angry I sounded.

Beagle didn't flinch. "Did you or did you not tell me I looked like a beagle?" he said.

"Well," I said.

"And are you or aren't you calling me Beagle in your head right now?"

"Well." I looked away.

"Look." Beagle smiled again. "Dani, I've got a little sister. She's awesome. I meant it nice. Okay? No offense."

"I'm not *anybody's* sister." Tears welled up in my eyes. Beagle ignored them.

16

"Okay, little brother," he said. "Eat this gorp like a good boy, then let's head up. We're close to the top now."

Here is the thing about missing Springer. It comes to me all of a sudden, out of nowhere, like a gust of wind that nearly knocks me down. I'm in the grocery store, say, or I'm standing in the middle of the busy school cafeteria, holding a tray of my favorite tuna and noodles, looking for a seat next to some friends, and I'm happy, I'm actually happy, not thinking about anything, and then *boom!* I miss Springer. I feel it hard in the pit of my stomach; I can't eat my lunch anymore. Or I eat my lunch and my friend Jane's lunch and then I pick leftovers off Tanner's plate and Caitlin's and Sarah's, because if I could just fill myself up I wouldn't miss Springer anymore.

And then I'm fine until the next time.

It happened on the summit of Springer Mountain. I expected that there'd be some kind of fanfare at the top, some elaborate marker like the pretty stone archway at the bottom of the approach trail. Maybe I wanted music and flowers just for me—maybe I was being unrealistic, since the summit was way in the middle of nowhere—but I expected more than I got, which was a big gray rock squatting beside the trail. I could see that it really did mark the summit—the trail went down from it in both directions—plus it had a metal sign stuck to it to mark the start of the Appalachian Trail, but it was just a rock like all the thousands of other rocks I'd already walked past.

"That's *it?*" I said aloud, even though no one was around, not even Beagle. He'd gotten ahead again. "*That's* the top of Springer?" It seemed stupid. For a second I felt cheated. But then I turned around.

Brown tree branches framed the longest, most beautiful view I'd ever seen. A few fluffy clouds floated high in a crystal blue sky, and far away on the ground a gleam of silver showed a river or a lake. On the mountaintop I felt suspended between clouds and water. The hills rolled on and on in front of me, green at their bottoms from evergreen trees and in some places showing the faintest pale green hint of spring.

Boom! I stood on top of Springer Mountain, and I longed for Springer. I stood with my mouth open, breathing in and out in hard, short breaths, and then I did something else I can't stop doing. I opened my pack and dug down the side, and pulled out an old T-shirt that belonged to him. I found it in my laundry basket a week after he died, and it smelled like him. It still does, the littlest tiny bit, even though I've kept it under my pillow all this time. So I stood on the mountaintop covering my face with an old unwashed T-shirt, and cried and cried and cried.

After a bit I heard man-made noises and jumped like a startled deer. It wasn't Beagle. It was a woman hiker, the one from the lodge, and she looked winded and sweaty and awful. Like the hike wasn't what she expected. Like she might turn around and go home. She walked up to the rock, glared at it, and said, "That's *it*?" and she sat down right on it with a thump and some creaks from her gear. Then she looked at me and said, "Oh, no! Are you hurt? What happened?"

I had quit crying, but I couldn't talk without hiccuping. I shook my head and tried to smile, and failed. "Nobody has to hike this thing," the woman said. "If it seems like a bad idea, hey, you know, they say a bunch of people quit right off the bat. Maybe that's fine, maybe you can learn as much on the approach trail as you need to know. Hey. How old are you anyway?"

I said, "Twenty-one."

She said, "My great-aunt Fanny. Don't tell me lies."

I said, "Twelve."

She sighed. "Well, you got the numerals right the first time, I guess. What are you doing this for? Please tell me you're day-hiking. You're not by yourself, are you?"

She was an older woman, like someone's grandma. Not mine, though. My grandparents were dead.

"Mmmm," I said. Just then Beagle showed up, walking back along the trail that led away from the rock.

"Hey, sis, I got water, need some?" he said. I shook my head. "Get a chance to sign the register yet?" he asked. I shook my head again. "Well, get a move on, supper's waiting."

"Where's the register?" I asked, and the woman said, "Oh, geez, I'm sitting on it," and we all laughed, and she signed it and I signed it, and she forgot I hadn't answered her question. Plus Beagle had made it seem like we were together, which was okay.

Beagle and I hiked the last part of the day together. We skipped the shelter just past Springer and went on to Stover Creek, so that by the end of the day I'd walked two and a half miles of the actual Appalachian Trail.

I ate dinner as fast as possible, ignored the other hikers as much as possible, and climbed into my sleeping bag as soon as I could. It was not even seven o'clock but I was exhausted, and I fell asleep before daylight had entirely left the shelter.

March 3
Stover Creek Shelter (Georgia)
Miles hiked today: 0 (so far)
Total miles hiked on the Appalachian Trail: 2.5
Weather: cold and windy

I woke to a blinding glare of light full in my face. A flashlight. I squinched my eyes and threw up my arm to block the light.

"Hello, Dani," my mother said very quietly.

I was trapped, caught, a girl in the headlights, unable to move in the face of oncoming disaster. I'd run away for what I thought would be six months but had escaped for less than two days.

"What do you have to say for yourself?" she said, again very quietly. Despite the flashlight, most of the other hikers slept on. I heard the rustle of a sleeping bag behind me that might have been Beagle, but no one spoke.

I said nothing.

"Dani?" she asked.

I could hardly see her behind the glare of light. I couldn't read her expression. I couldn't put a name to what I felt, either— mostly just another sense of loss. "What time is it?" I asked.

She flicked her sleeve back from her wrist. "Three-twenty-seven A.M. Scooch over. I'm freezing."

I scooched my bag closer against the shelter wall. "Not that way," she said. "Scooch over inside the bag." When I didn't move, she said crossly, "I've got to sleep somewhere, it's too cold without a bag. And somehow I forgot to bring one. I didn't expect to climb a mountain tonight."

I scooched. She burrowed into the bag with me. Her hands and face felt like ice.

"You climbed the approach trail in the dark?" I asked. I couldn't imagine it, not with all those rocks.

"Shhh," she said.

"But—"

"We'll talk in the morning. Go to sleep."

"I'm not quitting."

"Morning. Now sleep."

In my narrow sleeping bag she had to cup her whole body against mine, a mandatory full-length hug. Then she made it feel like a real hug, because she put her arm around me and let her face brush my hair. It seemed like years since the last time she'd hugged me. Since the day of Springer's funeral, the day Dad left, the day the world fell to pieces.

For a moment I thought about staying awake, sneaking out of the shelter once Mom was asleep, hoisting my pack, and taking off down the Trail. It wouldn't work, though. Impractical, for one, since I'd have to leave my sleeping bag behind. Impossible, for another. I hadn't even been sure my mother would look for me, but she'd found me right away. Running again would be useless.

Mom was sound asleep and her arm felt heavy against my ribs. Her breath was moist in my hair. Part of me felt little-girl safe in her embrace, but another part—a larger one—felt trapped like a bear in a cage.

We woke up angry.

"What were you thinking?" she asked. She ran her hands through her hair until it stood up on the sides. It was early. Some of the other hikers were still sleeping. Others had moved on. Those few awake near the shelter went about their business quietly, ignoring us, or pretending to. Beagle made coffee very slowly and didn't look at me. I hoped he wouldn't leave.

"Dani? Were you thinking at all? Did you realize what it would do to me, to come home and find you gone?" Her voice was quiet, her words furious.

"You can't make me leave," I said. Ridiculous, because of course she could. I knew that. I pulled my boots on.

Mom was sitting up in my sleeping bag. The morning air was ice cold. She wasn't dressed for hiking. She had a coat but no hat, blue jeans, a sweatshirt. All cotton, the worst fabric to wear. For a moment we stared at each other. I noticed that her hands were shaking. So were mine.

"Pick a question," she said. "Any question. And answer it."

"What questions?" I said.

"The ones I just asked you."

She had a hard, sharp face, my mother. She'd never gotten soft and round like other people's moms. She ran her three miles every morning in twenty minutes, every single morning, rain or sleet, always in the dark because she got up so early.

"I told you I was with Dad," I said. "I thought you'd believe me. I didn't think you'd *worry.*"

"Not at first, you mean," she said. "Not until you were too far gone to find. That's what you were thinking, right?"

I didn't answer. It was what I'd been thinking. Right.

She huffed. Her breath made a white cloud in the air between us. "I knew you weren't with your dad, Dani," she said. Something in her tone made my stomach hurt even more. "He's in Jamaica."

"Jamaica?" My dad was a wilderness kind of guy. He never, but never, went to the beach.

"He's getting married there," Mom said. "Our divorce was final last week, you knew that."

I couldn't talk. I couldn't breathe.

"I told you," she said. "I told you last week it was final."

I looked around the shelter. Everyone who couldn't seem to leave me alone the night before had moved away now. Even Beagle was out of earshot. "I didn't believe you," I whispered.

"Oh, Dani." She sounded exasperated. "Why not?"

They weren't supposed to get divorced. They were just upset about Springer. I knew they'd get back together eventually, when everything settled down. Married? My father?

"To who?" I said.

"Lisa," Mom said in a come-on-you-know-this voice.

I'd met Lisa exactly once, a few weeks earlier. Dad and I went out for pizza and she showed up at the restaurant. She had bleached hair and she spent the whole dinner picking the toppings I ordered off her pizza with her painted fingernails. "Dad said she was someone he had just met," I said.

"Oh," said Mom.

"So why is he marrying her?"

Mom answered carefully, like she was walking toward a land mine. "I think it was the right thing for them to do, considering that they're going to have a baby."

I put my hands over my ears and clamped my eyes and mouth shut.

"C'mon, Dani," Mom said, louder, so I could hear even

with my hands over my ears. Her voice sounded impatient and angry. "You had to know that much. It's obvious she's pregnant. She's almost five months along."

"I *hate* you!" I said. I uncurled myself, sprang up, fast, furious, and took off running through the woods. My boots weren't laced. I stumbled on a rock and fell facefirst. I lay flat, tight, holding myself down. It hurt, but I didn't make a sound. I'd had enough crying to last me.

I felt something wet run down my hand over my fingertips. Warm dripping blood, my own. I sat up. I'd sliced my wrist on a sharp rock, not deep enough to do real damage, but deep enough to bleed pretty hard. I wiped the blood away with my other hand.

Mom came down the path, her hands in her pockets and her collar up against the cold.

"It's your fault," I said. Not mine.

"Got a first-aid kit in your pack?" she asked.

"Sort of," I said.

"Got a stove?"

"Yes."

"Got matches?"

I did have matches. I'd taken three books of them from the restaurant at the lodge.

I turned my face away. "I hate you."

"Okay. Let's cook breakfast after we bandage your arm. I'm starving."

Mom didn't touch me as we walked back. She kept her hands deep in her pockets. I had to hold my bleeding hand elbow up so that the blood didn't get onto my clothes. Near the shelter I looked and looked for Beagle. I didn't see him anywhere. Where could he have gone? Was he finished already? Had he disappeared?

"Honey, is everything okay?" a woman asked us. I looked up. It was the same woman hiker I'd spoken to on the summit of Springer.

"No," I said.

"She's fine," Mom said.

"Can I help you?" she said.

"No," I said again.

But all I had for a first-aid kit were some antiseptic wipes and a couple of Band-Aids, and the Band-Aids weren't big enough for the cut on my wrist. The woman went through her own pack and came up with some gauze squares and adhesive tape, and a tiny foldable pair of scissors. She cleaned my cut with my wipes and wrapped her gauze around it.

"Thank you," I said.

"You're welcome," she replied. She looked at my mom and hesitated before asking, "Anything else I can do?"

Mom shook her head. "We're okay. I hope I didn't wake everyone up when I came in last night. Dani took off without telling us; we were worried about her."

"Who's *we*?" I asked. "Dad doesn't even know."

Mom gave me a sideways glance. "Of course he does. I called him."

"In Jamaica?"

You'd think the woman would've had her eyes bugging out of her head with curiosity by now, but she didn't seem all that interested. "I'm Vivi," she said to Mom. "That's my Trail name anyway. I made it up this morning. Sure you'll be able to get off this mountain okay? I could go with you."

Where is Beagle? I thought.

Mom blew out her breath and nodded. "We'll be fine."

I made as much oatmeal as my one pot could hold. It didn't taste a whole lot better hot than it had when I tried to eat it cold, but I was so hungry I didn't care. I took a bite and handed the spoon to Mom. I had only one spoon and no fork. I did have a Swiss Army knife. Hard to eat oatmeal with that.

Vivi had gone back to her own business with her own stove, but now she walked over again with a cup in her hands. "Coffee?" she asked Mom. "Your girl pack any?"

"I packed tea," I said. "But I can't boil water with the pot full of oatmeal."

Vivi nodded toward the cup. "Share that, then. I've got a bit left if you need more."

Mom sipped the coffee, then handed the cup to me. While I drank she spooned another bite of oatmeal. The coffee tasted like poison. "Tell me what you were thinking," Mom said. "Tell me your whole plan."

"I'm going to be in Maine by the middle of August," I said. "I'm going to climb Katahdin on the first day of September. I'm going to walk the whole way there."

Mom sighed and looked at me with heavy eyes. She took the coffee cup from me and wrapped her hands around it. "Why the Appalachian Trail?" she asked. I shrugged. She shook her head. "How much money do you have?" She gave the spoon back.

"Five hundred dollars. Almost." I ate and gave the spoon back.

She scraped the spoon around the edge of the pot. "So it was all your own money. You didn't take any."

"Of course I didn't! I wouldn't steal!"

"The only problem is"—she scraped the pot again and handed me a full spoon—"five hundred dollars will barely get you to Damascus. It's not nearly enough."

"I'll make it be enough."

"Honey, nobody's going to give you baby-sitting jobs along the way."

I flung the spoon into the empty pot. "You think I don't know anything, but I do," I said. "I can hike as good as you can. I read books about it. I practiced. I know all about it and I can do it, I can make it all the way, I know I can, and it's so rude of you to say I can't when it doesn't matter anyway. I know you're going to make me leave."

"I have to make you leave, Dani. You're not being rational. You're twelve years old, and anyway, people don't abandon their lives."

"Why'd you do it?" I asked.

"Do what?"

"Hike the Trail. You did it before. Were you abandoning your life?"

Mom stretched her feet out in front of her. She was wearing her good running shoes. They were covered in mud. "I don't remember," she said.

"Please," I said. "If you don't want to let me go by myself, come with me."

"I can't."

"You could if you wanted to." I sniffed. A big globby tear fell out of my left eye and pinged against the side of the pot. We both ignored it. "You just won't do it because I want you to."

"Katahdin." Whenever my mom used my full name, it meant I'd pissed her off. "What you want and what I want have nothing to do with it. I have a job, a mortgage on our house, an ex-husband—"

"Is he paying alimony?" I asked. "Is he paying child support?"

"He won't be paying anything if he finds out I've let you

run off into the woods," Mom said. "He'll be suing me for custody instead."

"You would have done it for Springer," I said.

It was a low blow, even I knew that. Mom's face went white.

"Don't ever say that again," she said. "Don't ever say that again."

"Okay," I whispered.

I poured water into the empty oatmeal pot and started to clean it. "And don't use so much water," Mom went on. "Water's precious, you've got to carry it and you've got to filter it. Just use enough to get the big chunks off the pot, then dry it good so it doesn't get germy. Here. Let me." She used her fingers to wipe out the pot. "Where's your towel?"

"I didn't bring one."

"No towel?"

"Just a little one. But I use it to wash my face. I don't want oatmeal on it."

Mom sat back on her heels. "Most people start a thru-hike with way too much stuff. You're the first person I ever met who started with too little."

"I didn't want to have more than I could carry," I said.

"Good thinking," Mom said. She looked at me for a long time. "Why does it matter so much?"

"I don't know. It just does." I started to shove the stuff back into my pack, first any which way, but after a second's thought, more carefully. We'd still have to walk down the approach trail.

"Why hiking?" Mom asked. "What can you get here that you can't get at home?"

I shrugged.

"What if we stayed out here a few more days?" Mom said. "Just a few. Would that help?"

"How many?"

Mom blew out her breath. "You really exasperate me, Katahdin. God as my witness, you do." I didn't say anything. Vivi came back and Mom handed her the empty cup.

"Suches," Mom said. "It's the first town on the Trail."

"I know," I said. It was twenty miles away.

"Write it down, Katahdin," Mom said. "Pay attention. I'm going to walk twenty miles up frozen mountains in blue jeans and running shoes. *I'm doing it for you.*"

March 3
Hawk Mountain Shelter (Georgia)
Miles hiked today: 5.1
Total miles hiked on the Appalachian Trail: 7.6
Weather: sunny, cold

While Mom went off to do something in the bushes—pee, I guess, though I wasn't going to ask—I found Beagle. He'd packed his gear and was sitting behind the shelter with his eyes closed. "That's my mom," I said.

"Figured," he said, opening his eyes. "So you're busted, huh?"

"Not really. Sort of. We're going to Suches."

"Cool," he said. He stood up. "See you."

Don't go, Beagle, I thought. *Or let me come with you.* "Thanks for breakfast," I said. "I mean, yesterday."

He turned around. "Don't tell people you're all right when you're not, okay? Here's your mom, frantic, and yesterday you were saying she knew you were up here."

I didn't know what to say. I looked away.

He came closer and tapped me on the chin. "Hey, whatever. Right. Look, the Trail's been here seventy years. It'll be here a hundred more. It'll be here when you come back." He walked away.

Mom was going through my pack. "That's mine!" I said.

"Do you have an extra hat?" she asked.

"Why would I want an extra hat?"

She grunted. "Good question. Why would you? Where'd you get all this stuff? Did your father buy it for you?"

"I bought it," I said. "I didn't tell him anything."

Mom took off her shoes and socks, put on my extra pair of socks, and put her shoes back on. She rolled my sleeping bag and tied it with my tent, and strapped the whole thing onto her back. "If this doesn't work, we'll take turns with the pack," she said.

"How'd you find me?" I asked.

"You left enough clues," she said. "There's a program on the computer, I can see what sites you've been visiting—hiking, hiking, hiking, Trail, Trail, Trail. Good thing, too. I was afraid you might have met someone online—one of those creeps in a chat room—I was so *afraid*." For a moment her voice trembled. "You still have no idea, the meaning of this, what you did to me. I can see you have no idea."

"You're mad at me," I said.

"Of course I'm mad at you! What mother wouldn't be?" She nodded at my pack. "Put that on. Let's get going. Long walk today."

"One who didn't care," I said, looking at the ground.

"What?" She'd lost it already, stopped paying attention.

"Never mind."

Sometimes I thought her eyes were steel marbles, the way she could glare. "There's not a mother on earth who wouldn't care, Dani," she said. "Not a single one."

Stomp, stomp, stomp, away she went. I hurried after her

31

but I couldn't catch up. She had less to carry than I did, and she was strong.

We'd gone a quarter mile down the Trail when we ran into a man walking the wrong way. He had a pack on his back—a full, towering, overstuffed pack—and he was sweating hard. His breath sounded like a bellows. I stepped aside to let him pass. I stared. I knew he was one of the ones who hadn't made it, who'd quit right there at the start.

Mom started to let him go by, then held out her hand. "Hey," she said. "You headed back to Amicalola?"

"Ma'am," the man puffed. "I surely am. This was the stupidest of all stupid ideas that ever came into my head."

"Can you take a message?" Mom scrabbled in her coat pockets and came up with a ballpoint pen from the bank. She searched a bit more and found an unused Kleenex in the pocket of her jeans. "Call this number, and leave a message on the machine. Say that Dani's found, she's fine, and we'll be in touch soon. Say it's from Susan. Okay?"

The man held the Kleenex delicately in his gloved hand. "This number, Dani's fine, from Susan. No problem."

"Thanks." Mom pulled out her wallet, but the man waved it away. "It's important," Mom said.

The man smiled. "Then I won't forget." He wheezed away, limping.

"Quit staring," Mom told me.

"I just can't believe anyone would quit. If you let me do this I would never quit."

But even with Mom carrying part of the gear, it took us three hours to walk five miles. It was not a particularly difficult section—downhill a good part of the way, and then a long, slow climb over a mile or so. It was a good deal easier than the hike up Springer the day before. But now my muscles hurt and I could feel a blister starting on one toe; my knees ached and so did my shoulders. Mom walked slowly, too, limping a little after she twisted her ankle on a rock. I worried about her wearing blue jeans; the books said not to because of the risk of hypothermia. Once we walked past a sign that marked an old cemetery. I didn't look. I didn't want to see the graves. We ate raisins twice. By eleven-thirty I was starving.

"Any water anytime soon?" Mom called out. She was behind me, hiking more slowly now.

I stopped and turned. "I've got some in my bottles."

Mom caught up to me. "If we hit a source soon, we can make something hot for lunch and have a good drink. How far do you want to go this afternoon?"

I took out my map. The hiking store at home sold beautiful topographic maps for every section of the Trail, but they cost a pile of money—the full set was more than my pack and tent combined. I'd bought the ones for the first section only. After that, I hoped I could borrow some, or maybe learn that I didn't need them.

Mom looked over my shoulder. We were almost to Hawk Mountain Shelter, which was near a stream. After that it was eight miles to the next shelter, Gooch Gap, and four more past that to the road that led to Suches.

Mom sighed. "So we're tenting it tonight, eh? I doubt I can make it to Gooch Gap."

I folded the map and stomped ahead. I knew I could make it to Gooch Gap. I could make it to Katahdin. No matter where we stopped tonight, we'd be in Suches tomorrow.

At Hawk Mountain Shelter we ran into Vivi again. She was hunched down watching the pot on her stove. "A watched pot never boils," I said, then bit my tongue.

Vivi smiled. "It'd better," she said. "I'd hate to have to eat noodles raw."

When Mom came up, she and Vivi fell to discussing Trail cookery like it was the main task in their lives. Vivi didn't ask why Mom was in blue jeans or what we thought we were doing, with one pack for the two of us. I supposed she'd overheard everything at Stover Creek. I got busy cooking lunch.

Mom broke away from Vivi. "How much food do we have?" I showed her my food bag. She nodded. "Plenty."

I said, "We don't even have to eat, we're only going to be out here until tomorrow."

"Three hours ago," Mom said, "you were pretty happy about being out here until tomorrow."

"Not happy," I said. "I wasn't *happy.*"

Mom looked at me for a moment and then went back to Vivi, who was having trouble with her stove. I took off my boots. My left sock liner had bunched up down by the toe, and that was causing what felt like a blister. I took both pairs of socks off. It wasn't a full blister yet, just a red spot on my skin. My right foot was okay. I put the socks back on, carefully pulling them smooth.

Vivi was telling Mom that a lot of faster hikers had gone past her. "Did you see Beagle?" I asked.

Vivi looked up. "Which one was Beagle? The one you were hiking with yesterday?"

Mom swiveled to face me. I couldn't interpret her look. It wasn't happy. "Um, yeah," I said. "I wasn't actually *with* him. . . ."

"Didn't see him," Vivi said. "He's not too old, is he? About your age?"

"He's a lot older than me," I said. Mom looked ticked.

After lunch we rested for half an hour before we got going again. Vivi left us behind. "What did you think of the hemlocks?" Mom asked.

"What hemlocks?"

"Hemlocks? This morning? Those great big trees?" Mom sighed. "You do know what a hemlock is, don't you?"

"Who was going to teach me that?" I asked. "Dad? You?"

Mom held up her hand. "Okay. Those big trees this morning, right after the shelter, those were hemlocks. That's the biggest stand of virgin hemlocks outside of the Smoky Mountains park."

"Oh," I said.

"Did you notice the big trees?" Mom asked.

"Not really," I said.

"How about the log bridge? The cemetery?"

"I noticed the cemetery," I said.

"We were both quiet for a moment. Then Mom asked, "Who's Beagle?"

"Somebody I met the first night."

March 3
Justus Creek (Georgia)
Miles hiked today: 11
Total miles hiked on the Appalachian Trail: 13.5
Weather: dark, cold

"What are you writing?" Mom asked.

We were both inside the sleeping bag with the zipper pulled halfway up and Mom's coat thrown over us like a blanket. It was very hard to move. I scrunched forward, aiming Mom's flashlight onto the page. "It's my journal," I said.

"I didn't know you kept a journal. That's a good idea."

"It's not a real journal," I said. "It's just mileage, where we stopped, what the weather was like."

"You ought to keep a real journal," Mom said. "That would be interesting. You could write about this afternoon."

"What happened this afternoon?"

Mom shut her eyes. "Everything," she said.

What happened was just hiking, lovely, plain, pure hiking. We came off Hawk Mountain and followed a ridgeline for a long time where we could see for miles through the bare trees on both sides. We weren't far from a road but it wasn't a busy road, and it felt like we were halfway to the sky. There were no clouds anywhere. We kept a comfortable pace. My feet weren't hurting anymore and my muscles were warm and loose; my heart beat steadily and strong. When we had to climb Sassafras Mountain, I did start to sweat, but I liked the feeling. I drew the cold air into my lungs. I felt whole.

At the top I sat down on a log in the sun and waited for Mom. Her shoes were making it difficult, I knew. The trail itself was a narrow ribbon of earth; the cold night combined with the sun's warmth had made it soft and slick. The soles of my boots left deep marks, but I didn't slip like Mom did.

When she came up, she dropped herself onto the log and let the makeshift straps of the tent and sleeping bag slide from her shoulders. I handed her some raisins and some water.

"Thanks," she said.

"Trade you," I said. "The pack for your stuff, for the next leg."

"Deal," she said. "It's pinching my shoulders." She looked through the trees with a hint of a smile.

"Was it this pretty when you walked it before?" I asked her.

"Mmmm," she said. "It gets better later on. It gets *green*. And then in September, in Maine, the leaves are red and gold."

I was sure that was true but it made me angry. "I want to see it," I said, "for myself."

"I know you do," Mom said. "Ready to move on?"

We climbed Justus Mountain, which was shorter than Sassafras, and then we were tired. We pressed on a bit to a creek and a good place to set up our tent, and there we found

Vivi, setting up hers. Her face lit up when she saw us. "Oh, my," she said. "Staying here tonight? I'm sure I'll get used to it, tenting by myself, but I didn't feel quite safe alone this first time."

Mom smiled. It was such an uncomplicated smile that I was shocked by it. It was like seeing the ghost of my former mother, the one I had when I was a little girl, before we knew Springer was sick. I turned away, my hands trembling.

"Dani?" Mom said. "You want to set up the tent while I filter water?"

"Sure," I said in a halfway normal voice. I wiped my face on my sleeve and went to work.

But when it came to lighting the stove, I hesitated. "Maybe we could have a campfire?" I said.

Mom said, "Oh, geez, Dani," which meant no, but Vivi said, "Wouldn't that be wonderful!" and started to gather wood.

"Check your guidebook," Mom said. "Make sure it's legal."

Campfires were forbidden in some places along the Trail but not in the national forest where we were. Vivi showed me how to clear a space in the earth and stack the wood just so. It was a lovely fire. We cooked our noodles over it and scorched the pot, and ruined my face towel using it as a dishrag. We didn't have marshmallows or hot dogs or anything you could cook on a stick. But Vivi shared some chocolate, and we all sat quietly watching the flames. I could have stayed up all night. At eight o'clock Mom said it was time for bed.

We got into the tent and then the sleeping bag. That was

when I took out my journal and Mom said I should write more than the date and miles. I didn't bother. I knew I wouldn't forget. I clicked off the light. Mom fell asleep. I reached into the side pocket of my pack, pulled out Springer's shirt, and pressed it against my cheek. I fell asleep in a heartbeat.

March 4
Suches General Store (Georgia)
Miles hiked today: 6 (so far)
Total miles hiked on the Appalachian Trail: 20.0
Weather: chilly, windy, warmer in the sun

I sat on the floor of the Suches General Store writing the morning's mileage into my notebook and cramming Snickers bars into my mouth. Mom was on the pay phone outside trying to reach Dad. I could see that she was talking to someone. Her face looked grim. After my third Snickers, the dude running the store came out from behind the counter. "You planning on paying for those?" he asked.

I spread the wrappers flat. "My mom will, when she comes back in," I said. "See, I'm keeping track."

"How many you going to eat?"

"I don't know. It's time for lunch."

"You could get a sandwich or something," he offered.

"Maybe," I said. I didn't know what our plan was going to be. Mom's car was in the parking lot at Amicalola. I supposed she could call the Gainesville taxi service to take us there. Since I wasn't the one making us leave the Trail, I didn't plan to worry about it. I started on another Snickers.

"Hiking?" he asked.

Brilliant deduction, given my pack. "Sort of," I said. I could see my mom gesturing with both hands, the phone receiver jammed between her shoulder and her ear. "But I think we're done."

A moment later Mom walked into the store. She looked awful, grimy and sore, and her jeans and shoes were ruined. I felt achy and tired, but not hurt. I wondered if I looked as dirty as she did.

"You'll never believe it," she said, smacking her hands together. "Guess where your father is."

"Jamaica?"

She shook her head. "Amicalola."

"Oh, *no!*"

"You're not kidding. He's a little upset."

"Tough," I said. "He can be upset all he wants. He's the one that ran off and got married to some bimbo." I thought of Lisa and her ugly fingers. I reached for the last Snickers on the rack.

"Give me that," Mom said. "How many have you *had*?" She ripped the wrapper open and took a giant bite.

"Six," the clerk said. We looked at him. "She's had six," he repeated.

"I told him you'd pay," I said to Mom.

"I'm not paying," Mom said. "You're the one with the five hundred bucks. I've barely got anything left beyond my driver's license."

We paid the clerk to calm him down and then went outside. "I guess I feel like you must have felt when I showed up at Stover Creek," she said. "Busted."

"Yeah, except you didn't spend six months planning this, and you're a grown-up and can do what you want."

Mom looked at me sideways. "You really planned for six months?"

"Yes," I said.

"Starting when?"

"That day."

"Hmmm." She sat down on the sidewalk and pushed her hair away from her forehead. We never talked about That Day. We never had to. Springer was buried on the first of September, and when we got home from the funeral, Dad started to pack. Neither he nor Mom said a word. I asked questions but no one answered them. By nightfall Dad was gone. Later in the week he called and gave me his new phone number. He acted like it was a perfectly normal thing to do, like I'd been sitting around wondering only what his new number would be. Sometimes he called to see if I'd finished my homework, and on weekends we sat in his new apartment and watched TV. I didn't play soccer in the fall, and he didn't even notice.

The night we buried Springer I dreamed my brother was standing tall and strong on the top of a mountain. I'd always known what our names stood for. I knew what I had to do. The only way to put our family back together was to start over, at the place where it'd all begun.

"Why is Dad at Amicalola?" I said. It was beyond hope, really, that he'd come.

Mom sighed. "I think he must have cut his honeymoon short a few days. He knew you were missing, I'd called him at the resort. He came home Thursday, and then yesterday the man we met on the Trail called and actually talked to him instead of his answering machine. So Dad drove down this morning."

"Where's Lisa?" I asked.

"At home," Mom said. "I talked to her. Then I talked to

your dad on his cell phone. He's on his way. He'll be here in an hour."

"Can we have lunch?"

Mom waved toward the store. "Help yourself."

I whispered, "Do you think he really got married?"

Mom turned and put her hands on my shoulders. Her eyes looked straight into mine. "I am certain he got married. I hope his marriage will be a long and happy one. It stinks for you, Dani, and I am so sorry, but please remember that there is now another child involved."

I pulled away. "Why didn't anybody tell me the truth?"

"Cowardice," Mom said. "Guilt. Fear."

"I mean you, too," I said. "Not just Dad."

"I know," Mom said. "So do I."

I went inside and bought a sandwich and a little bag of chips. I ate an apple and drank a pint of milk from the dairy case. I used the toilet and washed my hands and face in the bathroom sink. It was worse that Dad was coming for us, or maybe better. I couldn't tell.

Mom came in and said to the clerk, "You stock socks, blue jeans, anything like that? A fresh shirt, maybe?"

He shook his head. "No, ma'am. Got some deodorant. Got some soap."

Mom nodded. "Well, that would be good." She came up to me. "Here I am, trying to be honest and up front with you. What if we take a week's vacation and keep hiking?"

I tried not to hope. "What do you mean?"

"One week," said Mom. "It's Saturday now. I'll get your dad to call my office and your school, I'll make it work out somehow. Your dad won't be happy, but I'll make him agree to it if this is something you care about. But it's only one more week. You've got to understand that, and accept it from the start."

"Okay," I said very quietly.

Mom's expression changed. "Honey, you don't have to. I'm sure it's harder than you expected. And if I get gear you'll have to carry more. Would you rather go home?"

"No," I said. "I'd rather go to Katahdin."

"You can quit anytime," Mom said.

"I won't quit until you make me."

Mom smiled. "A week is the best I can do. Take it or leave it."

"Take it," I said.

"Besides," she added, "two thousand miles is a long way. We've done about one percent of the Trail so far. It gets harder, not easier."

I crossed my arms and didn't answer. Mom touched my elbow gently. "It's the best I can do," she repeated.

"Okay."

"Are you happy?"

"No," I said. "But thank you for trying."

She sighed. "Dani, we can't do the whole thing. It's not possible. I'm giving you a week. Aren't you glad?"

A week compared to how much time she gave Springer, to how much time she spent working? A week. "Sure," I said. "To finish the whole thing we only need to walk three hundred miles a day."

Mom threw up her hands. "Go for it," she said.

March 4
Walasi-Yi Center, Neels Gap (Georgia)
Miles hiked today: 6 (so far)
Total miles hiked on the Appalachian Trail: 20.0
Weather: too hot in car, too cold outside

Dad wasn't happy.

His car was the first one in several minutes that we saw on the road in front of the store. He accelerated toward us, stopped with a screech in the first parking spot, threw the door open, got out, and wrapped his arms around me, all in one continuous motion, like a movie.

"Dani!" he said. "Are you okay?"

"Yeah." He smelled so comforting and familiar, a little bit like Springer's shirt.

Dad pushed himself out to arm's length while still holding my shoulders. "Why did you do this?" he said. "Why did you run away?"

I looked away. "How was Jamaica?" I asked.

Dad's face turned red. His mouth fell open. "Of all the childish tricks," he said. "Is that why you ran off? I wouldn't have thought—"

"No," I said. "It's not why I left. I didn't even know where you were because you didn't tell me anything about it. I did not 'run off.' I'm *hiking*." I thought that of all people he would understand.

"You had us scared to death, Dani—"

"She knows," Mom cut in. "We've been over that. I think she understands."

"Does she have any idea what could have—"

I couldn't stand them talking about me in front of me. I said, "I'm sorry you had to come back early."

Dad looked puzzled. "We didn't," he said. "We had always planned to come back on Thursday. Lisa had to work."

Really, I did not feel like speaking to him, not at all, not ever again. But I couldn't help myself. I said, "So. Did you decide to marry somebody you hardly knew at all, or were you lying to me when we ran into Lisa at the restaurant?"

Dad opened his mouth, shut it, then opened it again. Mom said, "Dani, get in the car."

I climbed into the backseat. They started yelling at each other even before I could slam the door. I turned my face from the window and plugged my ears with my fingers. I tried to recall the peacefulness of the walk the day before on the ridgeline. I couldn't.

When Springer was alive, we'd play backgammon when our parents fought. They tried to keep their arguments private, but we always knew. Backgammon was a good game, just interesting enough that we had to pay attention, but not so complicated that we couldn't listen for when the shouting stopped.

Springer liked Dad best, I know. Dad liked Springer.

After a while the car door opened. I unplugged my ears. Mom shoved my pack into the backseat beside me and got into the front passenger seat. I looked out the window. Dad had his back to us. He was talking on his cell phone. "He's calling Lisa," Mom said. "He's going to take care of things so that we can stay out here this week." She gave me a funny look. "I know you're angry—I do—but please keep a cork in it right now. You're not helping."

"Sorry."

Dad got into the car and put it in gear. I hadn't noticed, but he'd never turned the engine off. "Are you taking us back to the Trail?" I asked. That was good; Suches was two miles from the trailhead. We'd hoped to hitch a ride in, but no one had stopped.

"I'm taking you to Walasi-Yi," Dad said. "Your mother needs boots and a sleeping bag."

"No," I said. "We have to stay on the Trail."

Dad turned onto the road. "I have to have boots, Dani," Mom said. "I can't keep hiking in running shoes."

"No," I said. "It doesn't count as a thru-hike if you skip any."

"Dani," Dad said, "this is not a thru-hike. You are taking a walk in the woods."

The car sped up. I opened my door wide. I was on the passenger side. I could jump, probably, onto the grass shoulder. I grabbed my pack.

"Dani!" Dad grabbed the other side of my pack and braked hard. "Shut that door!"

I didn't. The car was almost stopped and I took a leap out of it, leaving my pack behind. I tumbled onto the shoulder, into the ditch. I wasn't hurt.

The car stopped completely. Mom walked down into the ditch. She watched me stand up. "You are not behaving rationally," she said.

"I hate him," I said. "I think I really do."

Mom didn't say anything, didn't touch me, didn't move. "Get back in the car," she said after a long minute. "Do not try anything like that again." She put her head in the open door and said to my father, "After Walasi-Yi, you'll take us back here. To the trailhead. Okay?"

Dad said a lot of words to her about spoiling the child, about therapy, and how I never behaved like this before, and how I was a danger to myself, but Mom's face was like a rock and all his words were just washing over it without changing it at all. I understood that we would come back to the right place on the Trail, so I got in. Dad said a lot more on the way to Walasi-Yi. I didn't listen to any of it.

Walasi-Yi Center, at Neels Gap, Georgia, is the only place where the Applachian Trail runs through a building. The building, not surprisingly, is a hiker's paradise. Mom got boots and clothes suited for hiking, a pack, and a sleeping bag. We emptied my whole pack onto the floor and went through it, deciding whether we needed a bigger stove or more water bottles, figuring out what we could share.

Dad watched and shook his head. "Wow. Good bare-bones hiking. Did your mom tell you what to pack?"

"I did it myself," I said. "No one taught me." I waited for him to realize that he could have taught me, or Mom, but he didn't say anything. I said, "I wanted to take more, but I was afraid I couldn't carry it."

"That's smart," said one of the employees, a woman who was helping us. "You should see the stuff we ship off from here every year. Folks have only walked thirty miles by the time they reach us and already they realize they're carrying way too much. Man came in here yesterday with an eighty-pound pack." She whistled.

"But you don't have any comforts," Mom said. She had emptied the main compartments of my pack and now she unzipped the side pocket. With a slightly puzzled look she pulled out Springer's T-shirt, and then saw what it was.

"I have *that*," I said. I reached for the shirt and Mom gave it to me. Her face was very pale. I held the shirt near my face and sniffed it, just out of habit.

"Is that Springer's?" Dad asked in a choking voice.

I missed him so much. I longed for my big brother. Dad took a step closer and suddenly we felt like a family again, a little triangle of people huddled around a dirty old shirt. I said, "I use it for a pillow. It smells like him a little." I handed it to Dad, but he didn't smell it. He stood very still and cradled the shirt in his hands.

"Better keep it in that side pocket," Mom said. "Keep it separate from your other stuff."

I had expected them to think I was crazy for carrying around Springer's shirt. They were so gentle and sad that I forgot for a moment how angry I was with them.

"You might want to get a bigger journal," Mom went on. "And you need a heavier fleece. We've been lucky with the weather. People can freeze to death easier than you think."

We picked out a tent for Mom, and a pack, and a second pot and spoon, and another stuff sack for food. I started adding up the price tags. Mom's boots were expensive, and so was the tent. My five hundred dollars wouldn't pay for the pile of gear on the floor. "Can we afford this?" I asked.

"We're going to need it," Mom said.

"But . . ." For years I'd been hearing about the stuff we couldn't afford.

Mom smiled in a way I didn't like. "You're picking this exact moment to be practical?" she asked. "You who want me to quit everything and walk for half a year? You've suddenly chosen to be aware of this one small piece of reality? Dani, I'm touched."

So much for family feelings. I started to stuff my gear back into my pack. I bit my lip. My face felt frozen. Mom came up behind me and touched my arm. It felt like an electric shock. I jumped away. "I'm sorry," she said. "That wasn't fair."

"I know a lot about reality," I said.

"We can afford the tent," Mom said. "We'll put it on my credit card. We'll work it out."

"But—"

"This is part of the reason we can only stay out here a week. I need my job. But we'll work it out."

I got the fleece but no journal. We got more food (and more interesting food), too. Dad barely said anything on the trip back toward Suches, but he looked at his watch several times. I knew he was thinking of Lisa, and all my anger came back in suffocating waves. When he came to where the Trail crossed the road, he stopped and we all got out of the car. He hugged me stiffly.

"See you," Mom said, keeping her distance from him. "We'll probably stop near Hiawassee, I think there's a hostel there. We'll get a ride back to Amicalola and pick up my car. Dani will call you when we're home."

Dad took his cell phone out of his pocket and held it out to her. "No, thanks," Mom said.

"You might need it," he said.

"We'll be fine."

"Really . . ." He tossed the phone across the gap between them. Mom moved her hand to catch it but missed. The phone smashed on the asphalt.

"Sorry," Mom said. Dad picked it up and fiddled with it, but it was broken. "We'll be fine. Don't worry."

"All right. Good-bye." Dad stood leaning against his open car door. Mom and I went into the woods. I didn't look back.

When we'd walked awhile and stopped for water, I asked, "Why didn't you want the phone?"

"Pain in the neck in the woods," Mom said.

March 4
Woods Hole Shelter (Georgia)
Miles hiked today: 12.7
Total miles hiked on the Appalachian Trail: 26.7
Weather: cold again

We climbed Big Cedar Mountain, full packs and all, and made it seven miles to Woods Hole Shelter as daylight was fading from the sky. I was stumbling tired. I'd fallen on the last downhill stretch, and my knee was scraped and bleeding. My hands and feet were freezing. Six people had already set up in the shelter, and one more came in on our heels. No Beagle. No Vivi, either. Bunk space for us, which was good. I didn't feel energetic enough to set up a tent. Mom didn't look energetic enough, either, and for the first time I thought about her walking so far in new boots.

"Feet okay?" I asked.

She nodded but grimaced. "A few hot spots. Glad we bought moleskin. I would have told you if we needed to stop. Get water," she added.

I looked around. "Spring's back that way," a woman hiker said, pointing. "You passed it."

"Thanks." I grabbed my water bag and bottle, and the filter.

Then I recognized her—she'd been one of the many hikers at Stover Creek Shelter, my first official night on the Trail.

"Hi," I said.

"Hey!" Her face lit up. "I was wondering what happened to you. Your brother passed me on the Trail yesterday, but I didn't see you. I was kind of worried."

"Brother?" I said. My heart fluttered queerly. Was Springer with me after all? I was never sure how I felt about ghosts.

"Beagle?" she said. "He called himself Beagle."

He was calling himself Beagle. So I'd named him, given him his Trail name. I grinned. "Yeah, Beagle, he's fast. I'm hanging back with my mom now."

"Cool," she said. "Family that hikes together, huh? Great idea." She held out her hand. "I'm Corinna. Still don't have a Trail name. I'm waiting for somebody to give me one."

"I'm Katahdin," I said.

She pulled her hand back. "That's your Trail name? Really?"

"No," I said. I looked back at my mother, who was fiddling with the stove. "She gave it to me. It's my real name. Since always."

Corinna looked amazed. "Guess you don't need a Trail name, do you?"

I thought of Beagle calling me sis and little brother. I hadn't liked either of those. "Guess I don't," I said.

We had been eating nothing but noodles, oatmeal, and gorp—all food I'd packed myself, so I couldn't complain—but for dinner Mom created a feast: chicken stew with tomatoes and spices and dumplings, vanilla pudding, hot tea. We had two pots now, and two spoons. Mom made the pudding in a zippered plastic bag with powdered milk and water. We cut the side of the bag and squeezed it into our mouths. One glob hit the side of my mouth and dribbled down my chin, then fell into the dust. Mom said, "That's a waste of good pudding."

I said, "Help yourself," and picked it up with my fingers and held it out to her. Mom laughed. I laughed, too. I don't think we'd laughed together for a year, but we kept on laughing until I thought I was going to choke. I wiped my mouth on my hand and said, "Don't you want to do the whole Trail?"

She said, "Yeah."

"Really?" She sounded like she meant it. "Then why don't we?"

She took the pudding bag away from me and kneaded it back and forth in her hands. "Money and logistics," she said. "Having lots of money isn't important, but having some money is. I don't want to lose our house. I want to be able to pay my bills. It's a freedom thing. Between Springer's funeral and the last medical bills and the divorce, we don't have much savings."

I dug my toe in the dirt. I was sitting on a rock near where Mom had set up the stove, a stone's throw from the shelter. Corinna was eating at a picnic table under the shelter's porch. I'd thought of inviting her to join us, but I didn't.

"Plus," Mom continued, "you can't just leave your life behind. You go to school, Dani."

"I thought I'd call it homeschooling," I said. Mom gave me a strange look. "I mean," I explained, "I did think about school, before I started. But if I made it to Mount Katahdin on September first, then I'd only miss a few days of eighth grade, and we could just say I was homeschooling. They wouldn't even know."

For a moment Mom looked like she wanted to laugh, and then she did laugh, covering her face with both hands.

"You are such an enigma," she said. "You take off in the

woods and have everything planned so well that sometimes I forget you are still a child. What did you think I would be doing for those six months? Sitting home by myself telling everyone, 'Katahdin's homeschooling,' when I didn't even know where you were? Oh, honey, that's hilarious. If I hadn't found you right away, your face would have been on milk cartons nationwide."

She kept laughing. I felt stupid. I really had thought that no one would care if I missed school. School was dumb; school was easy. But I knew Mom was right. "We could still say it," I said. "If we did thru-hike. Now that you're here."

Mom wiped her eyes. "One," she said, "we are not thru-hiking. I give you a week and you want to take two thousand miles." She was still smiling so I knew this was supposed to be a joke, but I didn't smile back. "Two," Mom said, "homeschoolers are actually supposed to be learning schoolwork. What do you think, you're going to stuff an algebra book into your pack?"

"We could just say it," I said. "I wouldn't actually have to do it."

Mom said, "That's the silliest thing I've ever heard."

We had never been a family that talked much. This conversation felt like more than the total amount we'd had all year. I was exhausted. I shut up and rinsed the pots and rubbed the spoons clean. Mom watched me carefully. "Happy?" she asked. I looked up.

"No."

She sighed. "But you want to keep hiking."

"Of course," I said. "Are you happy?"

She thought for a moment. "No. I forget what happy feels like."

"So why keep asking me?" I said.

March 5
Walasi-Yi Center, Neels Gap (Georgia)
Miles hiked today: 4 (so far)
Total miles hiked on the Appalachian Trail: 30.7
Weather: partly cloudy, warmer

Before lunchtime the next day we were back at Walasi-Yi. I couldn't believe it, given how long it had taken to drive there. "The car had to go around the mountains," Mom said. "We walked over them."

I felt a little foolish that I'd made such a stink for ten miles of the Trail. I looked at Mom. "It's okay," she said.

Mom did have a small blister by then, so she went into the center to get more moleskin and look at the sock liner options. I stayed outside. I stuck some money in the soda machine and sat down on a bench to have a drink. I was tired, but I liked feeling tired. I had slept well every night on the Trail so far. When someone sat down on the bench beside me, I didn't look up.

"I thought you'd been sent home," he said.

I turned so quickly I spilled my soda across my hand. *"Beagle!"*

He smiled. "Breakfast girl," he said.

I wanted to hug him, but I didn't move. I didn't know what to do or say. He looked exactly like I remembered him. "I thought you'd be a long way from here," I said. "Someone told me you were hiking fast."

He held up his arm, bandaged white from elbow to wrist. "I met a sharp stick too hard and too fast," he said. "I tripped going downhill. Twenty-six stitches. Amazing." He shook his head. "So I had to get the folks here to run me to the hospital, and then I had to stay and wash all the blood out of my clothes."

"Did you cut any tendons?" I asked.

He looked amused. "No, I did not cut tendons. The ER doc told me I hadn't. She said that was good."

"It is good. If you damaged your tendons or your ligaments, you wouldn't be able to move your fingers correctly."

He eased his arm onto his knee. I thought he should have a sling. "You going to be a doctor, little brother?"

"No. I hate hospitals. I'm never setting foot in another one as long as I live."

"Never?"

"Never."

He grinned. "So you'll just have your babies right out in the forest, like the bears and the birds and the butterflies?"

I said, "I'm never having children."

"When the time comes," he said quickly. "Years from now."

I didn't answer. After a moment's silence, I told him, "My mom said we could hike for a week."

Beagle stretched out. "Cool."

Nothing outdoors was green yet, but it still felt green, with the woods all around and the sun and crisp air. I felt like I could sit still forever. "Is your laundry done?" I asked. All my clothes were horrendous, but I didn't want to waste any of my hiking week on laundry. I'd looked up Hiawassee, and it was fifty-three miles away. That meant ten-mile days, which would be fine.

Beagle shook his head. "Hardly started. I had to wait on the machine."

"Does your arm hurt much?"

"More than I care to say."

My mother came out of the building. "This is Beagle," I said. "My friend Beagle."

Mom nodded and said hello. "Dani said you bought her breakfast," she said.

"No big deal," he said.

"We could treat you to lunch," Mom offered.

"That would be great," I said. "We could wait here until your laundry is done, and you could hike with us this afternoon."

Beagle looked uncomfortable. "Hey, sorry," he said. "I've got some buddies I met up with; they went into town and they're coming back to get me." After a pause, he added, "Come along with us, if you want."

"I think we'd better keep moving," Mom said. "Come on, Dani."

Something in her tone made me get up and adjust my pack and start walking, but I was ticked. "Bye, Beagle," I said.

"Bye." He looked like he couldn't remember my name.

"Katahdin," I said.

"That's right. Cool name. Bye, Katahdin. Good luck."

Mom headed for an outbuilding. "They have showers here," she said. "We're both taking one."

"We could have gone with him," I said.

"I don't think he looked like he wanted us to," Mom said. "He said he's got buddies. Probably a bunch of young guys. They're probably having a good time together."

I knew the truth. Beagle was happy to be in my company. It was my mother he didn't want to hike with.

"I called your dad to be sure he got home," she said. "He couldn't talk because Lisa was puking. He said she has terrible morning sickness. She puked the whole time they were in Jamaica."

"Oh, I'm sorry," I said with bitter sarcasm.

"She's your stepmother now," Mom said. "You might as well get used to her."

"Right," I said. I thought of Lisa's baby. A little half brother or half sister. A little nondefective baby. "What else did Dad say?"

Mom shrugged. "Honestly? I think he's jealous."

March 7
Post Office, Helen, Georgia
Miles hiked today: 9
Total miles hiked on the Appalachian Trail: 52
Weather: rain

Bull Gap, Corbin Horse Stamp, Cowrock Mountain, Hogpen
Gap, Sheep Rock Top. For the next two days we hiked through a
regular farmyard. Nothing happened. Beagle and his friends
camped near us the first night, then walked ahead. Mom's blister
healed. She was quiet. We usually hiked apart anyhow. The person ahead—usually me—stopped and waited every hour or so.
I was quiet, too. I felt more comfortable spending the days without words.

At Low Gap Shelter we ran into Vivi again. She seemed
pleased to see us, and she asked us if we wanted to go into a
town called Helen with her the next day. "I've got a food drop
at the post office there," she said. "Plus, I'm dreaming of a
night in a motel room and a meal I haven't carried on my
back."

Mom perked up. She seemed tired. "We could read a newspaper," she said. "We could call your father."

I didn't miss newspapers and I didn't miss Dad. "We could

get a pizza," I said. Some things you just couldn't cook on an alcohol stove.

"Probably we could," said Mom.

"Several," suggested Vivi.

It was raining and miserably cold. I didn't have rain gear but I did have a big plastic poncho, like a tarp, and so did Mom. It didn't help much. Rain dripped onto my pants and down my neck. My boots were so wet they squished. We were warm enough so long as we kept moving, but we felt chilled the moment we stopped.

"Think pizza," Vivi said encouragingly. "Think hot shower."

"I am," I said. I couldn't imagine staying that night in a shelter, much less a wet tent.

After nine miles we got to the road. A car came along and Mom stuck her thumb out, expertly, as though hitchhiking was her main and customary method of transportation. The car screeched to a stop. Mom walked up to it and stuck her head through the open window. "Get a ride to Helen?" she asked.

The man inside studied the three of us. "You thru-hikers?" he asked.

I said, "You bet."

So there we were in Helen, a surprisingly touristy little town. We went first to the post office, where Vivi picked up the box of home-dried food she'd mailed to herself, and I used the pay phone to call Dad. I stomped my feet to warm them and put my fingers in my armpits. Dad sounded sulky. "You have no idea how much work this is even with you only being gone a week," he said. "Your school says I have to write a letter to excuse you. A phone call won't do. Couldn't you have planned it better?"

"How's your new baby?" I asked. "How's your new wife?"

"Look, Dani, your timing was far from impeccable."

I said, "Maybe you should have stuck with the family you had."

He had a lot to say back to that, but I didn't listen. I held the phone out to Mom and we could both hear his voice rising and falling angrily. Mom started talking and calmed him down. Then she listened to him for a long time. I watched her face take on that rocklike bad-news look. I felt my stomach twist. When she hung up, I asked, "What's wrong?"

She said, "You shouldn't talk to him that way. He's your father. Everything is not his fault."

"It's true. He should have stayed with us."

Mom paused for a moment, pressing her fingers against her lips. "Let's talk about that later," she said. "Shall we?"

"Let's talk about it now," I said. Vivi looked up and the clerk at the counter stared.

"No," Mom said. "I've got some things I need to think about, and some things I need to say. I need to think first. Let's find a room, warm up, and have dinner."

Mom stomped out and I followed. Vivi hurried after us; Mom looked surprised when she caught up with us, as though she'd forgotten Vivi existed.

We found a cheap motel and split a double-bed room with Vivi. We all took showers and washed our underwear and socks in the sink, and emptied our wet packs of everything and hung our wet gear all around the room. I wished I had something to wear on my feet besides soaking-wet boots. I wished I had something to wear that was dry, but I didn't. Even my spare underwear was damp.

We went to a restaurant and ate several pizzas. I couldn't believe how hungry I was. Back at the room Vivi turned the television on, then quickly turned it off again. "Too loud," she said. "Already I'm used to quiet."

Mom handed her a newspaper section. I paced around the room. It was dark. The motel's wallpaper was old and depressing; the bedspreads were violently ugly. I took my wet socks off and rubbed my toes. I had prune feet, hideous. I searched the room for one piece of clothing that was reasonably dry, and finally put on my long underwear top. I shook out and turned over all the other clothes I'd laid out.

Then I lay down in bed, but the pillows seemed about six inches too thick.

"Mom?" I said.

"Later."

Vivi didn't talk. I noticed this about Vivi: she was often quiet for long periods of time. She was nice in a Grandma way, but what did we really know about her anyway? She could be an ax murderer.

Vivi said, "I'm going to call my son."

"How old is he?" Mom asked.

"Thirty-six."

I couldn't picture an ax murderer with a thirty-six-year-old son. I threw the pillow on the floor. I got out Springer's T-shirt and wadded it under my head. I covered my head with the atrocious bedspread to drown out Vivi's phone conversation, and went to sleep.

When I woke up, it was still dark. I wasn't sleepy anymore. Vivi was snoring in the other bed, but Mom was gone. I could smell coffee. I opened the motel door, and there was Mom sitting on the step outside. She was dressed. The rain had stopped and the sun was rising between layers of purple-gray clouds. Mom had a Styrofoam cup in her hand. "Good morning," she said. "If Vivi's up, tell her there's fresh coffee in the lobby."

I shook my head.

"I'm still thinking about one thing," Mom said. "But here's something you do need to know. Your father and I did not get divorced because Springer died. It's been difficult for us for a long time. We probably would have separated years ago if it hadn't been for Springer. Neither one of us could have handled caring for him alone."

A wave of hurt, red hot, rolled up inside me. I thought I might throw up. "So you stayed together for Springer," I said, "but you wouldn't do it for me?"

We checked out of the motel and ate breakfast and hitched a ride back to the Trail. I kept waiting for Mom to say something to contradict me. I kept waiting for her to tell me something different—that they might have stayed together for me, or even just that they loved me, or something, but she never did. She didn't say anything at all until six-thirty that night, when she caught up with me near Deep Gap Shelter, panting hard, and said, "It's dark already, Dani, can we stop for the night?"

March 9
Muskrat Creek Shelter (North Carolina)
Miles hiked today: 7
Total miles hiked on the Appalachian Trail: 78
Weather: still cold, sunny

Sometimes I felt like I wanted to talk. I'd walk up a steep section, panting hard and sweating even in a cold wind, and it would be like I wasn't even on the Trail. I wouldn't see the mountains or the trees, or even the rocks unless I tripped. My mind would be running like the engine on a race car, fast and furious, saying all the things I thought. *You never paid attention to me. You never came to my soccer games. You never let Springer come. You were always working, or taking care of him, or doing something for yourself. Never me. You stayed together for him. Not for me.*

I loved Springer and I missed him, and every night I was sorry I couldn't say good night to him and tell him about my day the way I used to, but even so when I was walking, I thought only about all the angry things I wanted to say to my mother. I would sit on a rock and wait for her, and think about what I should tell her. Then she would walk up, sit beside me, slurp water from the bottle at her waist. She'd hand me a snack, and I would eat it. "Ready?" she'd say.

"Sure," I'd say. And we'd start off walking again, me pushing ahead, my anger making me fast and strong.

Two mornings after Helen, I woke to find my water bottles frozen solid beside me and ice crackling along the inside of the tent. The air had a sharpness to it, a chill that took a few miles of walking to shake off. Along the Trail long fingers of frost looked like they'd pushed themselves straight out of the ground. They were beautiful and fragile. They broke when I touched them. "Look," I said when Mom came up to me. It was midmorning. The frost was still there.

Mom smiled. "You're finally starting to open your eyes."

I scowled. "What's that supposed to mean?"

She shook her head. "Sometimes I think you're not seeing anything that's more than two inches off the Trail. You may as well pay attention. You might never get to do this again."

"What do you know about paying attention?" I said. "You never did."

There. I'd finally said something.

Mom looked at me for a long moment. She took my hand in hers and led me down the Trail until she found a log we could sit on. She sat, pulling me down beside her. She unclipped the sternum strap of her pack, then her hip belt, and let the whole thing slide from her shoulders. I kept my pack on.

"I know we don't talk often, so please listen," she began. "You're twelve years old, and I know you feel that life has not been fair, and that I especially have not been fair. I remember feeling the same way, with much less reason, when I was twelve. My hope is that when you grow older, you will start to be able to understand.

"I missed a lot, Dani. I missed your preschool Christmas

program and the science fair contest where you got third place, and—"

"My soccer games," I cut in.

She sighed. "Your soccer games. Not all of them, but most of them. And I didn't take you hiking, you did that on your own. I didn't spend summers taking you to the pool, and you were in day care more than I wanted, and you've had to fend for yourself a lot. But the thing you need to understand is this: I did the best I could. Every day. I had a dying child, and he did die, and he took up a lot of attention that would have otherwise gone to you. I can't change that. Would you have wanted Springer not to have been born?"

I started to cry. "Of course not," I said. "But you didn't have to work. You were always working. You always complained about your job, but you never quit it."

"I couldn't," Mom said.

"You could, too," I said. "We didn't need that much money. We could have lived in a smaller house."

Mom kissed my forehead and wiped the tears off my cheeks. "I was the one with the health insurance," she said.

I sniffed. "So?"

"Honey, think about it," Mom said. "I never really wanted to work full-time. I never had a career, a job I loved to do. We had Springer, and then we had you right away. I was home with both of you, and that was good. I was happy. But we wanted to save some money and buy a house, so I took the job with the bank. You were in preschool. The health insurance at my job was cheaper than at your dad's, so I put you and Springer and me on it. And then we found out that Springer had muscular dystrophy, and we were stuck.

"He couldn't go back onto your father's insurance because

his MD would have been a preexisting condition, and nothing related to it would have been covered. And mine was such good insurance—it covered everything for him—we could go to whatever doctor he needed. We couldn't give that up. So I had to keep working."

She shook my face a little with her hands. "*I had to keep working.* Dani, his medical bills were enormous. This last time alone, with the pneumonia, it was two hundred thousand dollars for just two weeks. That's more than your dad and I make in three years."

"Couldn't Springer have had insurance if you quit?"

"For eighteen months," Mom said. "That's the law—we could have paid his premiums for eighteen months ourselves. But only eighteen, and we could never say, 'In eighteen months this child will surely be dead and won't need insurance anymore.' And we knew he would never get better. So we couldn't do it. I looked into it, believe me."

"It's not fair," I said.

"Which part?" asked Mom. "The part where you had a brother? The part where the insurance company paid out over a million dollars for the care of a child born with a fatal disease? The part where he died? Fair has nothing to do with any of it."

"I thought he was going to live, that last time," I said. I leaned against her a little bit.

"Me too," she said. "Me too."

We had spent the night near Plumorchard Gap Shelter, though the place was so crowded we slept in our tents. We had a pretty short hike ahead of us, only seven miles, and then we would spend our last night at Muskrat Creek Shelter. From there we were only four miles from the road that would take us to Hiawassee, and from there to home.

At lunch Mom said, "I've been thinking."

I had been searching through my pack for one last candy bar, but something about her tone made me freeze. I sat back slowly.

"I didn't know about this until I talked to your dad at Helen," she said. "I didn't know anything about it. But if we agree, it might give us a little more time."

I didn't have any idea what she was talking about.

Mom swallowed. "There was a life insurance policy on Springer."

"What?"

"Your grandpa—your dad's father—took it out when Springer was born. As a gift to us, or something. I guess he told your father about it. But your grandpa died right before you were born, and the policy got put in with some papers at the bank, and your dad never thought about it."

"Before Springer was sick," I said. Duchenne muscular dystrophy is a genetic disease, so Springer was born with it, but he was diagnosed late, when he was six years old.

"Right," Mom said. "It's not a bunch of money. It won't make us rich. But it would pay our house payment for a month or two, and our other bills. It doesn't cost us much to stay on the Trail. Your dad says if we want to use the money for this, we can. He's worried about you. He says he didn't realize how upset you were until you jumped out of the speeding car."

"It was a very slow-moving car," I said. "What about your job?"

"I'll need to make some phone calls," Mom said. "I maybe need to go home for a few days, set everything up, make sure we can do this. But the bank set out some new policies last year. One is that above a certain level, employees are allowed to take a sabbatical for a few months, for any reason. No pay, but you keep your job." She shook her head. "When they first announced the policy, I thought, 'I'll save mine until the end, until I need it to be with Springer.' "

Springer's disease was the most common form of muscular dystrophy. All his muscles were weak, and they got weaker and weaker as he grew older. Exercise made him worse, not better.

Even when I was little, I understood what this meant. Our hearts are made of muscle. Muscles pull the air in and push it out of our lungs. When Springer got weak enough, he would die, but we thought that would be when he was around twenty, not thirteen.

"What about school?" I said.

Mom tried to laugh. "We could always say you're home-schooling. I don't know, Dani, you'll probably have to go to summer school. You don't want to fail a grade."

"I don't care if I do."

"It's a big step," Mom said. "I've been thinking hard because I wasn't sure I wanted to do it, but I'm willing to if it's important to you."

"Can we make it to Mount Katahdin?"

"No," Mom said. "We can't. I don't remember the details of the sabbatical, but I don't think I can take off more than two months. We'll have to settle for doing what we can."

"Okay."

"Happy?" Mom asked.

"Maybe," I said.

We were sitting in a big clearing high up in the mountains. The air was crisp and the sky was bright, bright blue. Mom looked around and then grabbed one of my guidebooks and searched through it. "Thought so," she said, leaning back in satisfaction. "We're in Bly Gap. Welcome to North Carolina."

We'd hiked one state through.

That night at Muskrat Creek Shelter I checked the Trail registry. There's one at nearly every shelter. Most of the time they're spiral-bound notebooks with pens attached. Hikers can write down anything they want in them, and when one gets full, a Trail volunteer takes it away and sets out a new one. I don't know what happens to the old ones.

I had signed the register on Springer Mountain, of course—everyone does. Since then I hadn't bothered. I wasn't much concerned with the other hikers. But today as I turned the pages, a message leaped out at me, maybe because it had my name surrounded by a box of little stars. *Good night, Katahdin, wherever you are. Beagle.*

Beagle was thinking about me. He was looking out for me. I felt so happy and so excited that I wanted to run back to the last shelter to see if he had left me a message there, too. I didn't, of course. But I'd sure read the registers from now on.

"What are you smiling about?" Mom asked.

"Nothing," I said.

March 12
3326 Holston Drive, Bristol, Tennessee
Miles hiked today: 0
Total miles hiked on the Appalachian Trail: 83
Weather: sunny, breezy, perfect for hiking

Our house was less like a museum than I could have wished. For one thing, it smelled bad. Mom had taken off for Amicalola in such a hurry the day she found me missing that she'd left some frozen chicken breasts thawing out in the kitchen sink. They had changed color. There was chunky milk in the refrigerator, too, and nasty dishcloths hanging by the stove.

Mom opened the windows in the kitchen. She dumped the rotten chicken into a plastic bag and took it out to the trash. I started the fan running and sprayed some Lysol into the sink.

It was midnight. We were tired. We'd hiked to a road that morning, but it turned out to be more isolated than we'd thought. It took us a long time to get a hitch into Hiawassee, and a while to find a ride from there back to Amicalola. Then we drove the whole way home. "Quitting, eh?" said the man who took us back to Amicalola. "Can't say as I blame you. We see a lot of those so-called thru-hikers. Most of 'em quit."

"We're not quitting," Mom said a little testily.

"Okay, lady, whatever you say."

Mom looked aggravated. I thought it was funny. I patted her shoulder, and she jerked it away and glared at me.

"What's wrong?" I whispered.

She shook her head. "I don't think any of this is going to work."

We stopped for coffee and snacks three or four times on the way home, and by the time we got there she was jittery. "Get unpacked," she said when she came back from tossing the chicken. "I want to get our laundry going. Go upstairs and get all the dirty clothes from there, too."

"Can we do it in the morning?"

"No. Take a shower, too, before you get into that clean bed."

I unpacked and showered and then I went to sleep. When I woke up, it was past midmorning. I'd slept like a piece of granite. I padded down the hallway. Mom was flat on her back in bed, snoring. I went downstairs. Most of the laundry was finished and folded. All the mail and newspapers were stacked on the kitchen table. I went outside and brought in the morning paper. I moved the last of the laundry from the washer to the dryer and started the dryer. I thought about getting dressed but didn't really feel like it.

I called Dad. "I'm home," I said.

"Great!" he said. "Can I take you out to breakfast?"

I put on some jeans and a clean shirt. I thought about waking Mom, but she looked so worn out I just wrote a note and left it on her nightstand. It was Sunday, so she wouldn't be able to call the bank or get started on anything important. She might as well sleep.

I was waiting on the sidewalk when Dad pulled up. I went around to the front passenger seat, but it was full. Lisa was sitting there.

"Oh," I said. "Hi."

"Hop in back, sweetie," Dad said.

"Good morning," said Lisa.

I planned on hating her for a long time yet, but I thought she ought to be pretty sweet to me. She'd gotten Dad, after all, and she'd gotten a new baby; I'd lost my brother and Dad both. But she had a look on her face like I'd swiped something important from her. I wished she had stayed home.

Dad drove right to our favorite pancake restaurant. We used to go there all the time when Springer was alive. I ordered banana pancakes with nuts and whipped cream, and sausage and orange juice and milk and a side of hash browns. Lisa stared. "You can't eat all that," she said.

I stared back. "Sure I can. I'm hungry."

She shook her head, then looked away.

"Hiking burns up a lot of calories," said Dad.

Lisa didn't look back. Dad patted my hand under the table and said, "Order whatever you want, honey."

Of course I was going to order whatever I wanted. I always ordered whatever I wanted. It was just pancakes, not filet mignon.

Lisa ordered one pancake, plain, nothing on it, especially no butter. She was thin enough, but she didn't seem like a diet freak, so I thought it was a pretty stupid order. I didn't say anything. Lisa didn't say anything. Dad tried to fill up the silence with questions about my hike, but he asked them so quickly I could tell he wasn't listening to the answers.

Our food came. Lisa took one look at my plate, clamped her fingers over her mouth, and ran from the table. Dad said uneasily, "She's had a difficult pregnancy. Smells make her nauseous."

"She can't smell pancakes?"

"She's reacted unfavorably to a broad range of things."

I stuffed a sausage into my mouth. "Like me?"

Dad took a deep breath. "She's eager to get to know you. She's just having a bad day."

Right. I kept eating. Dad didn't eat. He looked nervously toward the bathroom. He checked his watch. "Would you mind going in there to check on her?" he asked at last.

"Yes," I said.

Dad looked surprised. He fidgeted with his fork. "She doesn't want me to," I continued. "She doesn't like me. I'm sure she doesn't want me watching her puke."

"Well . . . ," said Dad. After a pause he said, "I think she will like you. She doesn't know you yet. You don't know her."

"Whose fault is that?" I said. "You didn't tell me anything."

"It's been hard," Dad said. "For all of us. It'll get better."

I didn't know what to say so I just kept eating. Dad cleared his throat like he was going to say more, but Lisa came back then. She had washed her hands and face, but a puke smell hovered around her. She said, "Thanks for eating your sausage first, Dani. That'll help."

"Okay," I said.

When breakfast was over, Dad asked if I wanted to go back to their house with them. "I've got a lot to do," I said. "We're going to try to be back on the Trail tomorrow evening."

Lisa pursed her lips. "Are you sure you think this is a good idea?" she asked.

"Yeah, why not? The sooner the better," I said.

She turned and gave me this adult-to-small-impertinent-child look, and I realized she hadn't been talking to me. "Missing school?" she said to Dad. "It doesn't seem responsible."

"It's fine," Dad said.

"But I don't think—"

"It's *fine.*"

End of discussion. End of seeing my father. Total words spoken by Lisa directly to me: 16. Total words spoken by me to Lisa: 15. I won.

March 19
Rufus Morgan Shelter (North Carolina)
Miles hiked today: 11
Total miles hiked on the Appalachian Trail: 133
Weather: warm, very springlike

The Trail was packed. From the moment we got back on I noticed how the number of hikers had increased. "They're bunched together," Mom said. "Some started early but have been moving slowly. Some started later and are moving fast. Not very many have quit so far."

Mom spent the Monday at home dressed in business clothes, going to her bank and arranging things. I spent the day going through our packs and getting everything arranged there. I also went through the refrigerator and threw out practically all the food in it. We didn't need to leave another disgusting piece of meat. I stayed home all day. I kept thinking Dad would call. He didn't. Maybe he thought we were already on the road.

When Mom got home, she looked worn out. She took off her dressy shoes and rubbed her insteps.

"Can we leave right now?" I asked.

"Yes," she said. She went upstairs. I followed. She changed

into her hiking clothes and carefully put her work stuff away. Then she went from room to room, drawing curtains and checking wastebaskets. They were all empty. I'd done that, too.

"There's a bus leaving in half an hour," I said.

"Nancy's taking us," said Mom. Nancy was our neighbor, Mom's one good friend.

"Right back to where we left?" The Forest Service road was dirt, a goat track.

"She's got a Jeep, remember?"

So we drove toward the Trail in Nancy's Jeep. We stopped for dinner on the way, and it got dark. By the time we got to the Forest Service road it was raining and absolutely black. Nancy turned onto the road and said, "Nope. No way."

She parked and we spent the night right there, with our sleeping bags draped across us. Mom and Nancy laid the front seats back and I stretched out on the backseat. I don't know how Nancy felt, but Mom and I were fine—it wasn't any less comfortable than your average shelter. In the morning Nancy hugged me hard, then hugged my mother. "This is a sane, healthy thing to do," she said. "Remember that."

We were only about a mile from a shelter so we stopped there and made a hot breakfast. The shelter was full, but of course we didn't know any of the hikers there. Beagle and Vivi and all the other familiar faces would be thirty miles away by now, and I was sorry we wouldn't see them again.

When Mom wasn't looking, I checked the Trail register. I had to flip back a few pages, but there it was: a box of stars, and inside, *Good night, Katahdin, wherever you are*. It was signed with a big B, which I knew meant Beagle. He was still thinking about me.

We took it easy the first day out—only eight and a half miles—but Mom took the lead and seemed glad to be hiking.

At lunchtime she said, "You haven't even asked yet how everything went."

"We're here," I said.

"Do you want to know for how long?"

"No." Because to tell the truth, I was still hoping for Katahdin. I didn't want to tick her off, though, by saying so.

Mom sighed. "Two months. Sabbaticals can be from one month to a maximum of three, but they didn't seem very happy about my asking so I told them I'd take two."

"If you're allowed three, you should have taken three."

"Look, I took a week's vacation last week with zero warning, and they gave me extra time when Springer died, and I've had several years with lots and lots of sick-kid days. I'm not exactly their star employee."

"You work all the time."

"That's your opinion," Mom said. Her tone softened a little. "And it's my opinion, too, I'll be honest with you. But it's not their opinion. Okay?"

"If it's policy they can't fire you," I said. "You should have told them three months."

Mom took a swig of water. "I'm not sure I want three months of this. Did you see any of your friends when we were home?"

"No."

"Really? Not even Tanner? Did you call her?"

"Yes," I lied. "She wasn't home."

At Rufus Morgan Shelter, Sunday night, Mom said, "You want to go white-water rafting tomorrow?"

I was busy cooking. "No."

Mom came over to me. "Come on, why not?" she said. "We're a mile out from the Nantahala Outdoor Center,

79

tomorrow we'll be walking right through it. We can stop and go rafting and stay the night in the hotel, then restock Tuesday morning. It'll be fun."

"No," I said. "I want to stay on the Trail."

"I've always wanted to go white-water rafting."

"So let's come back some other time," I said. She looked stubborn. I poked the noodles I was cooking with a spoon. "You had your turn on the Trail," I said. "This is mine. I want to hike."

"Dani," Mom said.

"No!"

The next morning Mom walked into Nantahala wearing her stone face. We started our clothes in the Laundromat there, walked to a grocery store a mile down the road, and stocked up for another week. We moved our wet clothes into dryers and paid to take showers, and we were back on the Trail by noon. "It's too cold for rafting anyhow," I said, once we were well on our way. "The water would be freezing."

"Your problem," Mom said, "is that you can't see the forest for the trees."

I waved my arm. "Look," I said. "Nothing but trees."

March 22
The Hike Inn (North Carolina)
Miles hiked today: 11?
Total miles hiked on the Appalachian Trail: about 160
Weather: blizzard

Although we were still not averaging more than ten miles a day, I was starting to feel really good. I couldn't tell if the constant aches in my muscles had really lessened or if I had just gotten used to them. My feet were tough; I rarely had a blister. I woke and ate, and hiked and ate, and hiked and ate and slept, and then did it all over again the next day. I didn't think about much, but I felt good. Mom quit longing for newspapers. Even when we had the chance, neither of us called Dad.

A few days after Nantahala we stopped for lunch at a shelter called Cable Gap. We usually ate cold food for lunch, apples and peanut butter and stuff like that, because it was too much trouble to dig the stove and pots out of our packs. Today, though, it was pretty cold and Mom wanted tea, and while she crouched beside the stove waiting for the water to boil, I leafed through the Trail register.

This time Beagle had written more. *All days are hard, but*

some are harder than others. Is Maine still part of the plan? Good night, Katahdin, wherever you are.

Of course it is, I thought. Maine was always part of the plan. I picked up the register's pen and leafed forward to an open space, and I wrote, *The Trail is the same, but the walk gets easier. Katahdin.*

There, I thought. It was a nice counterpoint.

That afternoon, it began to snow.

At first I was fool enough to think it was kind of fun. We were in a place called Walker Gap, nearly three miles past the lunch shelter and just over four miles from Fontana Dam, where, Mom said, we would find a pretty decent hostel with hot showers. Hot anything sounded good. I'd woken up cold and been chilly most of the morning. Now, between the wind and the wet sleety snow, I couldn't seem to get warm.

Mom looked at the heavy clouds, and she looked at our map. Then she looked at me. "This won't be easy," she said. "It's downhill all the way."

People think hiking downhill should be easier than hiking up, but it's not. Your heart pounds going uphill, but the rest of your body pounds going downhill. Your toes pound into the front of your boots, and all your other bones pound into each other. It hurts after a quarter of a mile, and soon you're wishing for a nice steep cliff to climb. Also, you don't fall uphill, or if you do, you're not so likely to slide off the mountain while doing it. With icy mud underfoot and my pack pushing against my back and shoulders, my hands shaking from the cold and my toes going numb, I started to feel that I was teetering on the edge of disaster with every single step. Reach—slide—grab—rebalance; reach—slide—grab—rebalance. As I grew clumsier I grew slower; as I grew slower I grew colder and clumsier.

Mom was in front of me. She turned and looked over her shoulder. "You okay?"

"I'm cold." My teeth chattered. The sky was dark and heavy. It clung to the mountainside like a thick wet blanket. Wet snow stuck sideways to the branches and trunks of the trees. It had started to accumulate on the Trail itself. My boots were wet through. I wondered how we'd get down this stretch once the rocks were covered.

Mom stood still while I made my way to her. "What clothes do you have that you aren't wearing?"

I blinked at her. "One shirt. Socks. A pair of shorts." I was wearing my thermal underwear and my fleece, and a hat and gloves.

"Put the shirt on. I'm going to find some sticks for us to use for hiking poles. We need to eat something, too."

By the time I'd gotten my pack off, my shirt on, and my pack back on, she was back with four big sticks. I rested my weight against one, and it snapped into two pieces. I looked down at the piece still in my hand.

My mother laughed. "Sucky day," she said. "We'll get through it."

"Want a Pop-Tart?" I asked. I threw the broken stick into the snow.

"You bet."

I cannot say for sure how we made it down that mountain. Within twenty minutes of our stop I felt twice as miserable as before. I fell once, ripping my thermal pants across the knee and bruising my knee, too. Mom kept on, faster than I wanted her to go. My teeth were chattering and I really wanted us to stop again, put up our stove, and make something hot to drink.

When I said so, Mom shook her head. "We're too wet. We'll freeze if we don't keep going," she said.

I knew she was right, but I didn't want her to be right. I knew we needed to keep moving, but I wanted her to slow down. I knew I had no reason to be angry with her, not that day at least, but I was.

Then she fell. On the trail below me I saw her stumble, try to catch herself, and roll forward in what seemed like slow motion. The Trail followed the ridgeline, and she went right over the side of the mountain, rolling and crashing into trees. She didn't shout. She came to a stop and didn't move.

I threw myself forward, skidding, sliding, fighting to keep upright and still run down the slope. When I reached her, she was on her stomach in the snow, her face turned a little to one side. "I'm not hurt," she said.

"Are you sure?" I asked. My heart pounded.

"No," she said, "but I think so. Except I can't get up." She'd landed stomach down with her feet uphill, her pack on top of her and her arms and legs tangled in the sodden underbrush. I helped her roll over and stand up. She was scraped and filthy. Blood trickled down the side of her face, and when she took a step she winced.

"Is it bad?" I asked.

"I can't tell yet," she said. She picked up her walking stick and took another step, and another. "Not horrible," she said. We climbed back onto the Trail. "Not good," she admitted. Her lips were blue and she was shaking. "And now I'm really wet," she added.

I pulled out the map and tried to guess where we were. "Long way yet," I said. "Let's go."

Now it was my turn to push, my turn to lead. Mom gritted her teeth and kept walking. I stayed just in front of her. I made her swallow some water and eat a candy bar. I kept careful watch for the white blazes that marked the Trail. I checked the map, and I decided when we could rest for a moment and when we had to move on. Mom looked awful, and the sky was getting darker. The nearest shelter was still two miles away, but at the end of the unholy mountain was a road. U.S. 28. I tried to remember what day of the week it was, and wondered if anyone would be out driving in the snow. Mom's eyes were looking glassy, and I couldn't feel my feet. I thought we needed to get under shelter, and soon.

Finally, the road. I made Mom take off her pack and sit on it, and I laid my own pack against her to shield her from the snow. After a moment I unlashed my sleeping bag and draped it over her. She had stopped shivering, which was not a good sign. I was shivering so hard I felt like my eyeballs were bouncing loose. Not a good sign, either.

A solitary car swung around the bend in the road. I stuck out my shaking thumb. The car kept going, then braked hard, its wheels sliding on the wet road. It turned around. It pulled up next to us, and the driver inside reached over to open the passenger door. She looked out. "Lord, you're not thru-hikers?" she said. "Get in!"

I helped Mom heave her pack into the backseat. The car was an old one with wide bench seats. Mom and I crowded into the front seat, where the heater was. I was still shivering. Mom looked blue.

The woman driving didn't seem put off by our sodden filthiness. She turned the heater up full blast. "Wait a minute," she said. She got out and rummaged through the trunk, and came back with an armful of old towels that smelled like dog pee. "Wipe yourselves dry," she said. "It'll be about a fifteen-minute drive in this weather."

"But the shelter's that way," I said, pointing over my shoulder in the direction she'd originally been driving.

The woman shook her head. "I'm not taking you to a shelter tonight," she said, "not in the shape you're in. Your mom's too cold, you know that?" I nodded. "So." The woman smacked her lips and nodded once, hard. "I'm taking you to the Hike Inn."

My mom stirred a little and smiled. "The Hike Inn. It's still there?"

"Yep," said the driver.

"Mmmm," said my mother. "Trail Magic."

Trail Magic is when you stumble toward a road crossing after a long afternoon of uphill climbs and find that someone—you'll never know who—has left a cooler full of cold sodas and fresh fruit there, with a sign telling you to help yourself. Trail Magic is people seeing you in a town with a full pack on your back and offering you a ride back to the Trail. And Trail Magic is when an untidy woman finds you at the end of the scariest afternoon of your life and takes you to a place that's safe and warm. The Hike Inn was like heaven after that day.

By the time we got there Mom had started to shake, and the woman driving us wouldn't leave until she'd seen Mom safely into a room, lying down swathed in blankets with hot water bottles—our water bottles, filled with the hot water from the tap—at her feet and hands, and the room furnace running full tilt. "You take care of yourselves now," she said, cupping my chin in her brown hands. "Stay here until the snow melts, don't be fools. And have fun." Then she tucked a piece of paper into my hand and walked out into the snow. The paper was a business card: Mandy Dennis, Attorney-at-Law. I put it into my pack next to Springer's shirt. I stripped my wet clothes off and took the hottest shower I could stand.

When I got out of the shower, Mom was sleeping. Her cheeks and lips were pink again, and she looked okay. I found another blanket in the closet and tucked it around her, then put on the driest clothes I had (still pretty wet), bundled all the rest of our clothes with the hotel towels, and hauled the bundles down the hall in search of washing machines and food. There had to be hot food somewhere.

There were laundry machines, the desk clerk told me. There wasn't a restaurant but there was a pizza delivery service, and when I called they promised to bring three large pizzas with everything right away.

And there was Vivi. I couldn't believe it. The clerk had just finished saying, "Honey, how's your momma?" when I looked up and saw her coming down the hall. My mouth must have dropped open a foot.

"Dani!" Vivi said. "What happened? Do you need help?" She rushed over and put her arms around me. I was so relieved not to be alone anymore that I burst into tears. Vivi held me tight.

Vivi came back to our room and agreed with me that Mom looked all right. "Hypothermia is a dangerous business," she said. "You did a good job. You handled it well."

I shook my head. "It could have been so much worse. If that attorney hadn't been so good to us . . ." My voice trailed off.

Vivi pushed the curtain back from the window. We were sitting at the little table by the door, eating pizza. Vivi had already eaten but was glad to have just a little more. We had saved one whole pizza in its box for Mom. Vivi said, "This is nasty bad weather. I hope everybody got off the mountains."

I took a swig of the Coke I'd bought out of the machine. I felt almost cozy. Vivi had lent me dry socks and a fleece sweatshirt so that I could put mine in the washer. "Why is everybody so helpful?" I asked.

"You mean on the Trail, or in general?" asked Vivi.

"On the Trail," I said. "Mom and I hardly talk to people, but they're all still nice to us. At home we don't even talk to our neighbors, except Mom's friend Nancy. When Springer died, they didn't even know."

Vivi answered slowly, "I think out here we're more aware of how much we need each other. If I abandon you today when you need help, maybe someone else will abandon me tomorrow. But if I take care of you, then you can take care of someone else, or someone else might take care of me.

"It's a community of strangers," she said. "A neighborhood that extends two thousand miles."

That night I dreamed Springer and I were running races in the grass. The field was wide and full of yellow dandelions; the sun was warm and the air smelled sweet. I was wearing my sundress with red poppies on it, my favorite dress when I was four years old. Springer wore his soccer uniform, blue shirt, black shorts. We were running across the grass, racing, laughing. He stumbled and fell, and I ran into Daddy's arms, yelling, "I won again! I won again!" Springer got up, a puzzled look on his face, and said, "Why do I keep falling down?" My mother glanced at my father quickly, then looked away. I knew something was wrong.

It wasn't really a dream. It was a memory. The next day Mom took Springer to the doctor. The day after that was his sixth birthday, and the day after that we took a long ride to the Knoxville Children's Hospital, and they told us Springer had Duchenne's. A nurse led me down the hall to get special lollipops out of a big glass bowl. I chose carefully, one for me, one for Springer. I remember thinking that the right flavor of lollipop would make Springer better. I was really stupid then.

I woke up in the dark room and found that I was leaning against my mother. Her breathing was soft and regular, her body warm. I snuggled closer to her and went back to sleep.

March 26
Mount Collins Shelter (Great Smoky Mountains
National Park, Tennesee/North Carolina state line)
Miles hiked today: 13.5
Total miles hiked on the Appalachian Trail: 199
Weather: cold high up, muddy, snow melting

Springer walks and runs in my very earliest memories, but in all my later ones he is weak, far weaker than me. He couldn't push his own wheelchair—his arms were never strong enough. From the time he was eleven he used an electric-powered chair. Springer could not lift a regular baseball bat, let alone swing one, so when we played in the yard he used a hollow plastic one. He could not throw a regular basketball, but he could throw a lighter ball, though never high enough to make a basket. He needed help to get his schoolbooks out of his back-pack. Using a pencil made his fingers tired.

Here on the Appalachian Trail, I grew stronger every day. I carried thirty pounds on my back, up and down mountains, over rocks, in the cold wind and hot sun. I no longer felt achy at night. Mom was as fit as I was, and we walked farther every day. We ate often, as much food as we could hold.

It was odd to think of someone like Springer, all the prob-lems he had and all the things he could not do, and realize that he came from my mother, who looked so healthy and strong, but who carried Springer's disease in every one of her cells.

Odd to think how I might carry it in mine.

We had rested a day at the Hike Inn, until Mom's sore ankle felt better and the snow had begun to melt. Vivi stayed with us. Like us, she'd gone off the Trail for a few days: She'd flown to Baltimore for her niece's wedding.

"It was good," she said. "Gave me a chance to see my kids, gave them a chance to see me. They're all for Mom's little adventure, but they can't help worrying some." Vivi laughed. "My youngest nephew kept saying, 'But you said you were going to be a thru-hiker!' He couldn't understand that thru-hikers didn't have to hike nonstop."

Mom let out a snort. I didn't say anything. I tried to picture Vivi's kids. "Do you have grandchildren?" I asked.

"No," she said, "but my daughter got married over Christmas. So maybe I'll get some soon, the good Lord willing and the creek don't rise."

We left the Hike Inn to enter the Great Smoky Mountains National Park, and right away it seemed like a different sort of Trail. There were rules to follow about where we could sleep and what we could do. The shelters were packed, and not just with thru-hikers, either, despite the still-chilly weather. The open fronts of the shelters were all caged with mesh fence, to keep the bears out, and even if we had to tent, we were supposed to store our food inside the shelters.

"Do bears make you nervous?" I asked Mom.

"No," Mom said. "I saw bears the first time. They eat garbage. They don't eat people. At least, not often."

At Derrick Knob we met a guy named Trailhead. He was a high school teacher, about Vivi's age, and he started talking to her at dinner and then he started talking to me. "Look at that!" he said, watching me boil noodles. "She cooks dinner for herself, without being asked!"

"She eats dinner herself, without being asked," I said.

"Can you filter water, too? Can you sling your food bag into the trees?"

I glared at him. "She's got dead aim with a carbinger," Mom said. Carbingers are little metal doodads that can clip stuff to your pack. We tied one to our rope to weight it so we could throw it over a tree branch more easily. It was true I usually hung the food, because Mom was pitiful at it. I cooked more often, too, because Mom didn't like the stove. Mom fetched most of the water.

"I'll have to take your photograph," he said. "I teach high school English, and a self-sufficient adolescent is something of a miracle to me." He bugged me, and I guess Mom could tell.

"Self-sufficiency is made, not born," she said.

Something in her tone made Trailhead back off. He talked a little bit about himself then; he was from some Podunk town with no hills. "Land so flat you can stand on a stump and watch the earth curve away," he said.

"Sounds awful."

"Damn sight easier to hike, though."

This broke everyone up laughing. By the end of the evening I liked Trailhead pretty well. "You're thru-hiking?" he asked me. "You and your mom?"

Mom was listening. "Kind of a section hike," I said, "but it's a long section."

I kept checking the Trail registers. Beagle's notes were getting more mysterious. At Fontana Dam he wrote, *Hiking in snow is a miserable experience. Wet and cold. Good night, Katahdin, wherever you are.*

I couldn't argue with that, but I wrote, *The mountains look beautiful under blankets of snow. Today I saw green shoots poking up from the ground. Spring will come soon. Katahdin.*

"Spring is here," Mom said in my ear. I jumped and covered the registry with my hand. Of course she didn't see what Beagle had written—he was a few pages back, a week ahead of us now.

"That's private," I said.

Mom raised an eyebrow. "Then save it for your journal, not the registry. It's spring, Dani. The first day of spring was a week ago."

"Whatever," I said.

March 28
Cosby Knob Shelter (Great Smoky Mountains National Park, Tennessee/North Carolina state line)
Miles hiked today: 13
Total miles hiked on the Appalachian Trail: 216.5
Weather: sunny, no breeze, warmer (mid-60s)

We arrived at the Cosby Knob Shelter on our last night in the Great Smoky Mountains National Park to find that a troop of Girl Scouts had taken it over. You would think that since there are campgrounds scattered throughout the Smokies, Girl Scouts would use them instead of shelters designed for thru-hikers. You would think that if they decided to stay in a shelter, they would show consideration for people who were obviously on the Trail for more than a weekened, and not, perhaps, take over the entire thing. You would be wrong. They built a big fire and spread their mess all over the one picnic table. They tore branches off trees to use as hot dog roasting sticks. They did not notice when half a dozen thru-hikers muttered angry words in their general direction, packed up their gear, and left. They were lively Girl Scouts. They sang a song about squashing bumblebees.

Mom and Vivi and I were not exhausted, but we were tired. We finished our dinner right about the time the Girl Scouts started theirs, and now we wanted to sleep.

"How far to the next shelter?" Mom said, eyeing the troop.

"Eight miles," I said back. Mom groaned. We couldn't go that much farther—we'd be walking until midnight. But in the park you weren't supposed to set up tents away from the shelters. "We could go maybe half a mile," I said.

Mom shook her head. "Better not." The Girl Scouts, gathered around their campfire, began another song.

Vivi grinned. "If you need something for earplugs, I've still got clean socks."

We set up our tents on the edge of the cleared area and climbed in. I'd gotten used to sleeping in shelters with strangers. I'd gotten used to weird smells and weirder noises, grunts, whistles, and the scamperings of mice in the dark. I had not gotten used to Girl Scouts singing.

I got out of my tent and walked over to the fire. I had planned to say, politely, something like, "Would you mind keeping it down a bit? Those of us who are serious hikers are trying to sleep," but as I approached the group I realized two things, and I held back. The other girls were my own age. And they all looked happy.

One of them noticed me. "Hi!" she said. Her ponytail swung perkily. "You aren't lost or anything, are you? Is your troop somewhere around?"

I was wearing a short sleeved T-shirt over a long-sleeved T-shirt and the tights I usually slept in. I'd hiked all day—several days, actually—in both shirts, and hadn't taken either one off when I'd gotten into my sleeping bag. The Hike Inn had been our last laundry opportunity, and these were the cleanest clothes I owned.

"I'm with my mom," I said. "We're camping in those tents over there." I pointed into the dim light.

"Neat!" said Perky Girl. "I wish my mom would come hiking.

I just love it, don't you? I love camping out. I love this shelter. We walked almost four miles from the Cosby campground to get here. We had to carry all our food and *everything*!"

I nodded. "I've gotten kind of used to that," I said. "We're hiking the Appalachian Trail."

Perky Girl nodded, *uh-huh*. "How long is that?" she asked. A few of the others looked up, and an adult who was with them saw me and started to walk over. I looked at the loaded picnic table. They'd brought food enough for an army. How they'd carried it four miles was a mystery.

"Two thousand, one hundred and sixty-seven miles," I said. Chocolate. They had chocolate on the table, and marshmallows, and graham crackers.

Perky Girl started to nod again, then made a choking noise and looked up at me, thunderstruck. "Two *thousand*?" she said.

I said, "I've done two hundred so far." They seemed like nice people, and not just because they were interested in me. They gave off a friendly aura.

"You must be a thru-hiker," said the adult, who I guessed was the troop leader.

Which I suppose should have been the cue I needed to say, "Yes, and so are the other people who might have enjoyed this shelter but are sleeping in tents because you took it, and who are being kept awake by your thoughtless giggling and noise." But once again I was stopped by two things: the thought that they did get to the shelter first and so didn't kick anyone out of it; and the s'more shoved into my hand by Perky Girl. "You must be starving," she said, wide-eyed. "Come sit by the fire."

When I weighed myself on the hiker scales back at Walasi-Yi, fully clothed, the needle hovered just below 105. "Good God," my mother had said, "you're already losing weight." She gave me a speech about the number of calories consumed by walking up and down mountains carrying thirty pounds on your back for eight hours every day. "I'm eating," I said. "You know I am." She did know. "You're going to have to eat more," she said.

The truth was I was almost always hungry. Two hours after eating an enormous meal, I was hungry again. I had never been heavy, but now my pants hung loose and my hip bones chafed against my pack belt, and as my mom reminded me often, we still had a long walk to go. So I ate, and ate, and ate, lots on the Trail and more at every town. That night around the Girl Scout fire I had over a dozen s'mores. I think there was half a chocolate bar in each one. They were delicious.

The Girl Scouts all seemed interested in hearing about my hike. They told me about their troop and the town they came from, the school they went to, how much hiking they did every year. I said, "My mom and I, we're taking some time away." I did not say what we were getting away from. I looked toward the tents, and there was Mom, rubbing her eyes sleepily as she approached us.

I got up to go. The troop leader introduced herself to Mom, and before I knew it I was eating yet another s'more while three of the Scouts toasted marshmallows for Mom.

The fire flickered, and the chocolate tasted smooth in my mouth. Mom sat down on a log near the fire. I sat down on the ground beside her and leaned against her legs. She pulled my hair back from my face with both her hands. The warmth from the fire felt like a blanket around us.

In the morning the Girl Scouts slept late while we intrepid thru-hiker types pushed out early. There were several people in tents on the fringes of the woods. One woman, whom I'd seen for several days running but not ever spoken to, gave me a nasty look when I ran into her at the spring. "Why is it you can talk to those Scouts half the night and ignore the rest of us?" she said. "Would it kill you to be friendly?"

I blinked. Mom and I kept to ourselves, sure. Why should anyone care? "I suppose it would depend on who was friendly with me," I said.

"Well, I guess," she said irritably. "I don't suppose you'd have anything to fear from me."

Except that I might catch your attitude, you old bat, I thought. I said, "There aren't many people out here like me."

"Solitary, you mean? Hermits in the woods?"

"Twelve," I said.

The woman nearly dropped her water. "Oh, wow, are you? Well, no wonder you don't talk much, I suppose. I never knew a twelve-year-old who did. But I'm surprised at your mother, you think she'd be dying for a chat after a long walk all day. I know I am. I never thought I'd hear anything as quiet as these woods. Have you ever seen such a place for being by yourself all the time? I know I haven't. When I get to a town, I head straight for the busiest place I can find. I just want to hear words so bad. I miss television, don't you? You must, a kid like you. What was your mother thinking, dragging you on this kind of a trip? You must be plumb miserable."

By this point we were back near the shelter. I said, "The trip was my idea," and dove into my tent. I hoped she'd leave. Instead she introduced herself to Mom ("Flutter, that's my trail name, some men I hiked with the first week gave it to me, don't know why, they were in some kind of hurry, they went on ahead"), and the next thing I knew she was offering to hike with us and pool our food for lunch. ("I know I'm sick and tired of everything that's in my pack, I bet you're sick and tired of everything in yours. We could share—just like grade school.") I shot out of my tent and started sending Mom signals behind Flutter's back, and mouthing, "No. No, Mom. Say no."

Mom said, "Oh, *shoot*," with such vehemence that it sounded like a swear.

"What's that?" Flutter asked, licking her lips nervously.

"We can't do that. I'm sorry." She turned to me and said, "Pack up fast, Dani. We've got to run."

I packed up fast. When we were well under way, with a dazed-looking Flutter left behind us, I asked, "Why are we in such a hurry?"

"Because," Mom said, "if I have to share the washing machines at Mountain Momma's with that nitwit I will lose my mind."

"But we lost Vivi," I said.

"We did not. She had her tent down already. She'll be up with us by lunch."

April 2
Rich Mountain campsite (Tennessee/North Carolina state line)
Miles hiked today: 9
Total miles hiked on the Appalachian Trail: 278
Weather: mild—leaves budding out on trees

We took a zero-miles day at Hot Springs, North Carolina. It was the first real town the Trail went through, and as Mom said, we needed a real town. We needed groceries and clean clothes; I needed to have one of my boots repaired; Mom said she needed "a decent cup of coffee, and maybe later a beer."

"What about a newspaper?" I teased her.

She grinned. "I'm thinking more along the lines of a really good book."

We got a hotel room across the street from the outfitter's and took my boot to be repaired. Mom bought me a pair of sandals for walking around town in. They were wonderful, so much lighter than my boots. Mom watched me walk for maybe half a block, and then she turned us around and bought some sandals for herself. She went to the bank and found a phone to check her answering machine messages, and spent some time making phone calls. I went outside and watched ducks walk on the lawn. We found Vivi and went out for a big dinner. Then

Mom said, "They've got white-water rafting here. Are you still against it?"

I said, "We've got a lot to do tomorrow."

Mom sighed. "How do feel about renting a Jacuzzi?"

"What?"

"They don't call it Hot Springs for nothing."

So we walked to the spa and rented a big hot tub, Vivi too, and sat in it for an hour. It was heaven. Vivi said, "You know how when you're really hungry and then you get to eat something good, it's the best feeling in the world?" I nodded. On the Trail, that was a feeling I had all the time. "That's what this spa is for my muscles. I walk and walk—but then there's this."

I thought of what Beagle had written in the registry at the outfitter's. *This town is paradise, or maybe I just miss civilization. It's hard to contemplate getting back on the Trail. Good night, Katahdin, wherever you are.* He had written it only a few days before, so I guessed he must have gotten held up somewhere. I wrote, *Towns are useful but ordinary. I love the extraordinary Trail. Katahdin.* Mom didn't see it. I didn't tell her about it, either.

"Have you called your father?" Mom asked. She knew I hadn't.

"Tomorrow," I said.

"You have to call him," she said. "He misses you."

I missed him, too. I missed him being home with us, with Mom and Springer and me, the way our family used to be. I didn't miss the version of my father that sat in some new house watching TV with his new wife, or hanging wallpaper in the new bedroom for his replacement child. "Whatever," I said. "I'll do it tomorrow."

I didn't. We were at the Laundromat and I asked for change

to use the pay phone outside. I went to the phone and pretended to dial and talk.

"How was he?" Mom asked.

"Fine."

Heading out of Hot Springs, we ran into Trailhead, who'd stayed at the Jesuit hostel. He told us he'd been there a few days, resting his left knee, which had started to hurt and swell. Now he hiked with it wrapped in a dirty Ace bandage, and he'd slowed down a bit so he was moving at about our speed. We had a fairly easy day, but dark came early, helped along by a bank of black storm clouds.

Lightning began shooting out of them and we could smell the rain coming. We had just passed the summit of Rich Mountain. It would have been a good night for a shelter, but we were two miles from the closest one. We pitched our tents near a spring recommended in the guidebooks, making sure they were as secure as possible. We hurried dinner and finished as rain began to fall in driving sheets. I started to duck into my tent.

Vivi grabbed my arm and pulled me back. "Come on," she said. "Susan, you too."

"Where?" Mom asked.

"Trailhead?" shouted Vivi.

"Forget it," he yelled from inside his tent.

We'd seen him limping the last mile. Mom shook her head, and Vivi called to him, "We'll be back in a bit."

She led us back along the trail we'd just come down. Rain poured upon us, and the trail became a stream, but Vivi bent her shoulders and walked fast, and we followed. After a bit she dodged onto a side trail I'd seen earlier, and not too much farther along we reached the base of a fire tower—a tower used by rangers to look for forest fires. Lightning flashed; thunder boomed. Vivi started climbing.

I thought first that in a thunderstorm you were supposed to stay low; I thought second that the fire tower probably had lightning rods or something, was probably safer than the trees. The storm grew fiercer as we reached the top. We were high enough that we probably could have seen for miles if we'd been able to see anything at all. It would have been neat in daylight. I was wet to the skin.

Lightning illuminated our faces; Mom was smiling, and Vivi's eyes were wide and happy.

"This might not be the smartest place to be right now," Mom said.

"It's my anniversary!" Vivi said, almost shouting as the wind picked up and rain blasted the tower.

"Of what?" Mom shouted back.

"Of living!" Vivi said. "I've been cancer-free for exactly two years!"

She hadn't ever mentioned cancer before. I'd felt reasonably happy, but now my mood crashed to earth like a kite caught in the storm. Geez, I was sick of people dying. Or nearly dying, or thinking about dying, or probably dying.

"Hooray!" Mom shouted. She caught Vivi up in a hug, the rain crashed around us, and she and Vivi danced a wild jig on the mountaintop while I stood and watched them, soaking wet.

The only good thing I could think about the whole excursion was that I had been wearing my sandals, not my hiking boots, so my boots stayed dry. I was so drenched by the time we got back to our tents that the only thing I could think of to do was strip naked, fling the clothes I was wearing over a bush, and crawl into my tent. Trailhead was in his tent, and anyway it was so dark no one could see me. I toweled off with part of my sleeping bag. I stretched out on my Thermarest pad, pulled the damp bag over me, and thought about getting a dry T-shirt out of my pack. Before I could finish the thought, I fell asleep.

At breakfast Vivi sat next to me. Trailhed was still in his tent, and Mom had gone off to pee. "You look upset," Vivi said quietly.

The campsite had some logs where we were sitting. It was chilly and overcast, and my clothes were damp. A stiff wind kept blowing my granola off my spoon. Finally I gave up and ate it with my hands. "That's just the way I look," I said.

"I've learned that the word *cancer* can scare a lot of people," she said.

"It's not that." I tipped the bowl up and drank the milk out of it—nasty stuff, made from powdered milk and water. "I'm sorry," I said. "I don't mean to be rude. I'm just really sick of hearing about people dying. I've had a whole year full of it, and I don't want to think about it anymore."

Vivi looked at me earnestly. Her entire face seemed to shine. I noticed the deep wrinkles around her eyes and mouth, the way her hair was mostly gray. "It's not about dying," she said urgently, as though it really mattered. "Look around you. Everyone is dying, every single person that you see. It's about *living*."

I made a noise that came out more like a snort than I had intended.

"It's a tough world," Vivi said, not seeming put off. "It's got to be hard to be your age, too, and have to think about these things. Most kids don't have to. Most kids think they'll live forever, and you know better. So make your life count. Enjoy it. Don't spend time doing things you hate."

"My mom did," I said.

"Because she had to," Vivi said. "She didn't have a choice. But now she does, and you see what she's doing."

"Walking."

"It's nice that you two are so much alike," she went on. "What you both need most is right here. Your mom can take care of you and herself at the same time."

I had never once thought of myself as like my mother, not in any way. Nor did I think she was actually taking care of me. I hiked with my own feet, didn't I? I asked, "Did she tell you about Springer?" I sure never had.

"Some," Vivi said. "It's still hard for me to get a picture of him as a person." She paused. "What was he like?"

It took me a moment to find the words. "He was really funny, but most people didn't realize it because he was so quiet about it," I said. I set my bowl down and plucked a piece of grass. "He'd say something in a completely serious voice, and then later, when you weren't even around him anymore, you'd realize he meant it as a joke, and it was funny. He was good at art and he liked bright colors." I twisted the grass in my fingers. "He used to say that if he had muscles, he'd be a cowboy, a real one that roped cattle."

Suddenly I could remember his voice, the way he said "roped cattle" so seriously. We had been watching rodeo on TV. His voice had deepened in the months before he died.

"When I was little," I continued, not looking at Vivi, "I used to be scared of thunderstorms. Really scared. I'd wake up crying and couldn't go back to sleep. Dad didn't like it that I was afraid, he'd tell me there was nothing to be scared of and I should go back to bed. So once I took my pillow and my blanket and I went down to Springer's room.

"I stood in the doorway, crying. He turned his head and said, 'What's wrong, Sissy? Are you afraid?' I told him I was.

105

He told me to lie right down on the floor next to his bed. 'There,' he said. 'Now you're with me. Now you're safe.' "

"And you were," Mom said. I hadn't noticed that she'd come up behind me.

I nodded. "And I was."

We were all quiet a moment and then Vivi said, "I notice you're not afraid of thunderstorms anymore."

"Why bother?" I said.

She smiled. "I agree."

"Is your cancer why you're hiking the Trail?" I asked.

"Probably," she said. "I'm in remission, but I'll never take time for granted again. I've gotten sharpened up. I realized I always wanted to do this, and I'm not waiting anymore."

April 8
Unicoi County Memorial Hospital, Erwin, Tennessee
Miles hiked today: -4
Total miles hiked on the Appalachian Trail: 341
Weather: normal

We walked on. At No Business Knob Shelter, which we passed through Friday morning on our way to the Nolichucky River, Beagle had written, only three days before, *Sometimes I think I have No Business being out here. Good night, Katahdin, wherever you are.* I didn't know what got into Beagle sometimes. I wrote, *Mostly I know we have No Business being anywhere else. Katahdin.*

We hitched into Erwin, Tennesee, for supplies. Mom and Vivi and Trailhead and I ate a monster dinner at the Kentucky Fried Chicken's All-You-Can-Eat Buffet. ("They must turn pale when they see hikers coming," Trailhead said, licking his lips.) Then Mom and Vivi and I wanted to stay in a hotel, but Trailhead decided to go back to the Trail. He had taken a semester off from teaching, but he had to be home for the start of classes the last week in August. He knew exactly how many miles per day he needed to average to make it, and he was getting worried because he'd fallen behind. Mom told him not to worry, he'd hike farther later on when his body was stronger. But I think we were all worried, because his knee was getting worse. Anyway, Trailhead left and we went to sleep.

In the morning Mom pointed out that the Nolichucky River had white-water rafting. I said, "Why would we want to do that?" She looked like she wanted to argue with me about it, and to be honest I probably would have let her win—I was tired of hearing about it and the day was pretty warm—but for some reason she kept quiet and we moved on.

Down by the river it was nice and flat, but then we started climbing, and after a few miles we came to one of the steepest slopes we'd climbed so far. It was a real lung-buster, and the fact that the weather had suddenly gotten hot didn't help at all. We all had hiking poles by now, and so we grabbed hold, dug in, and kept climbing. By the time we reached Curley Maple Gap Shelter, four miles from the river, we were bushed.

"Lunch," I said.

We took off our packs and our boots and ate some real bread with some lovely fresh cheese. Bread doesn't keep well in backpacks, so a few days after a grocery stop we were always down to stale bagels and crackers. Cheese doesn't last long, either, but that's partly because I eat it all up.

Mom reached into the top of her pack with a big smile. "Here," she said. She opened a little plastic box of strawberries. They shone like red jewels. I put one in my mouth.

"Oh, my," I said.

Vivi took one next, and then Mom, and then me again. We ate them one by one until they were gone. *Beagle,* I thought, *I wish you could be here for this.*

We started walking again. The Trail was flat for nearly half a mile, along the ridgeline of a mountain, and then it started up again. We had only gone a little way when we found Trailhead, doubled over in agony on the side of the Trail, clutching his knee.

It was his right knee, his *good* knee, and he'd done something horrible to it. He told us he'd tripped and thrown his weight sideways to try to save his sore knee, and instead his other knee had twisted beneath him as he went down. He'd hurt himself a few hours ago and had come a quarter mile back down the Trail on his own, little by little, dragging his pack. "I was afraid to dump it," he said, "I didn't know when someone would come. I thought I might be out here all night."

We gave Trailhead a pole and helped him to his feet. He couldn't put any weight on his leg at all. His muscles were shaking and tears ran down his cheeks. Mom supported him. "Can you hop?" she asked.

"Have to," he said. He hopped and she held him up. He hopped again. I thought of that treacherous uphill climb—it would be worse going back down.

Mom had taken off her pack. Counting Trailhead's, that left Vivi and me with two each. Trailhead's was heavy. "Suggestions?" asked Vivi.

I couldn't see leaving any of the packs unless we had to. Who knew what we would end up needing? Who knew how long Trailhead could hop? "Drag them," I said.

We used our hiking poles to extend the frames into travois. I took some of our bungee cords and turned them into handles. We dragged the extra packs behind us. It dug up the Trail, which I hated to do, but I didn't see we had much choice. I really didn't think I could carry seventy-five pounds.

Hop, stagger. Hop. Hop, stagger. Hop. Mom and Trailhead kept going. The hot sun beat through the thinly leaved trees. Hop, stagger. We made it back to the flat part, but the going didn't seem any easier. Hop. Hop. Trailhead's face was turning gray. We stopped and drank water.

Hop, stagger. Back to the shelter now. "Should I run ahead for help?" I asked. "Do you want to wait here?" It was midafternoon.

"No," said Trailhead. "Let's keep going." Mom looked at him. "Picture your average ambulance crew," he said. "Do you think for a minute they're going to be able to carry me down this mountain?"

"If it gets to be too much, say so," said Mom. She was sweating and grimy.

Hop, stagger. Hop. Hop, stagger, fall. At the start of the steep section, Mom and Trailhead went down. I couldn't tell who fell first. Trailhead screamed. Mom held him, helped him up. She looked so unsteady that Vivi traded places with her for a while.

Hop. Stagger. Hop. We had to be so slow, so careful. Hop. Stagger. I tried to take a turn with Trailhead, but I was so much shorter than he was that I couldn't support him. Mom took over. Hop. Stagger.

The pack I was pulling kept clipping my heels. I had to lean backward to stay upright, and my toes jammed against the fronts of my boots. I could feel blisters starting where I'd never had blisters before.

Then I saw the most welcome thing, a group of three other hikers coming toward us through the woods. I thought I recognized one of them. "Beagle!" I shouted. Below us, they looked up. Three men, but not Beagle. I swallowed my disappointment. "Help!" I yelled instead. "We need some help!"

They were stronger. They supported Trailhead more easily and could move him a little faster. They helped us pick up and carry the packs. When we got to the road, they helped flag down a car and told the driver to call an ambulance. They stayed right with us until the ambulance guy said he didn't have room to take us all to the hospital. "We'll handle it," Mom told them.

The men grasped Trailhead's hands and hugged the rest of us, and stood on the road watching as the ambulance pulled away. Out the window I saw them putting on their packs. I realized I'd never even asked their names, Trail or otherwise.

At the hospital emergency room they whisked Trailhead into a room and gave him some pain medicine right away. He was so exhausted he fell asleep. A nurse brought some paperwork to Mom. "I'm not his wife," Mom said. "I can't do that." The nurse suggested Mom just fill out what she knew. Mom said, "I don't even know his real *name*."

We waited and waited for news. Hospitals always made me nervous, especially emergency rooms, with their air of tragedy. I hated to wait for bad news surrounded by strangers all waiting for their own bad news. I hated the plastic chairs. I hated the bad magazines.

Mom reached over and took my hand. Vivi looked like she'd fallen asleep. I said, "Do you remember the day Springer broke his arm?"

"Yes," she said. He'd been eight years old. He'd just gotten his new wheelchair. He'd shot too fast down our driveway and the chair tipped when it hit the curb at the end. He wasn't wearing a seat belt, and he landed on his outflung arm.

"I pushed him," I whispered. "Down the driveway. I made him fall."

"I know," Mom said. "I remember." She stroked my hair. "You didn't know any better. You and he were playing. You both thought it would be fun."

"I didn't mean to hurt him," I said. That had been the first day I really understood that I could—the first day I realized that I was stronger than Springer, and always would be.

"He knew that," Mom said.

We sat for another hour, and someone came out and said Trailhead was asking to see us. He was wearing a light blue hospital gown and looked very dirty, very tired, and very, very brave. "I blew my ACL," he said. Mom winced. I must have looked confused, because Trailhead took my hand and explained that it was one of the ligaments in his knee. He said, "Time for surgery. I'm done." He took off the religious medal he always wore around his neck and handed it to Vivi. "Take that to Katahdin for me, will you?" He sank back into the pillows and closed his eyes. "Thanks. Thanks for everything. Don't worry, now. I'll be fine."

Mom said, "Your family?"

Trailhead didn't open his eyes. "Wife'll be here in a few hours. I'll be okay." As we started to walk out, he called, "Dani?"

"Yeah?"

"Thanks for letting me get to know you. I've enjoyed it."

"Okay."

We took up our packs and walked out into the cool night. Vivi said, "Got to be a motel near here somewhere."

Mom stopped suddenly and smacked her forehead. "What day is it?"

"April eighth." Vivi checked her watch. "Yep. About ten P.M. Why?"

Mom shook her head. "Taxes. I forgot all about the taxes."

April 9
3326 Holston Drive, Bristol, Tennessee
Miles hiked today: 0
Total miles hiked on the Appalachian Trail: 341
Weather: warm, raining

Vivi seemed to understand what taxes meant in a way that I did not. "Shoot," she said. "You didn't finish that before you left?"

Mom shook her head.

"It can wait a few weeks," I said. "Can't it?"

"Of course it can't, Dani," Mom snapped. "The federal government expects to be paid on time. And your father and I have to file together, we were married all of last year. I can't mess him up, too." She heaved a sigh. "Didn't Dad ever mention this when you talked to him?"

"Um," I said. I'd never talked to him, though I'd pretended to several times. We walked down the sidewalk, Mom muttering to herself and Vivi looking for a taxi as though there might be such a thing in Erwin, Tennessee, late at night.

"Dani," Mom said, "why are you limping?"

"I think I messed my feet up pretty bad."

I'd had blisters already, of course, but they had been the sort you could rub with alcohol, put some tape over, and ignore.

Mom marched me back to the emergency room. When I took off my boots, all ten toes were cracked open and bleeding.

"Oh, Dani!" Mom said. "Why didn't you say something?"

"They didn't hurt that much," I said.

Mom shook her head. "They will."

"I couldn't help it," I said.

"Of course you couldn't, baby. Well, you'll have a day off now anyhow. I've got to call your father and have him come get us."

"Now?" I said.

Mom looked exasperated. "It might as well be now. Have you looked at a map lately? We're only forty miles from home."

"We are?" The only maps I'd looked at were our Trail ones, precise, detailed renderings of mountains and valleys, with shelters marked clearly but hardly any towns.

"Erwin," Mom said.

"Oh," I said stupidly. "*That* Erwin."

"Oh, sugar," Mom said, rubbing my neck lightly. "I can't believe I'm putting you through this."

"You're not putting *me*," I said as I stood up, wincing. "I'm putting *you,* remember? This was my idea?"

"But I knew," she said. "I'm the mother. I'm so sorry about your toes."

A sympathetic doctor bathed my feet, rubbed them with antibiotic cream, and wrapped them in gauze ("We get a lot of hikers in here, you bet"). Vivi sat with me while Mom went in search of a pay phone.

When she came back, she looked furious. "Why didn't you tell me you hadn't talked to him?"

"You told me I had to," I said. "I didn't want to."

"But if you'd told me the truth, I would have called him myself. I would have let him know we were okay." She rubbed her forehead with her fingertips. "He's been frantic. He didn't know where we were."

"Of course he did!" I said. "We were on the Trail. He could have come looking if he was so upset." I thought of the Trail registers. "He could have found us. He just wants to fuss at us but not do anything himself. He gets to have everything his own way."

Mom shook her head. "He's your father."

I said, "Well, he's not a very good one."

"You're out here, aren't you?"

"Because of you. Not because of him."

Mom didn't know what to say. Vivi gave Mom's shoulder a little squeeze. "Want to come off the Trail with us?" Mom asked her. "Free hot shower, rest a day? It shouldn't take more than one day."

I suddenly thought that I might stop breathing if we lost Vivi right now. I didn't know why. Maybe it showed on my face. Maybe that was why Vivi nodded slowly, and said, "Sure. That would be fine."

Dad kissed me when he saw me. His face was furrowed with an expression I didn't recognize, and as he looked me up and down the furrows grew deeper. "You look awful!" he said. "You must have grown two inches taller. How much weight have you lost? Your mother said you hurt your feet. How bad are they?"

"Hi, Dad, nice to see you, too," I said. "I've got ten blisters and bad B.O. How are you? How're Lisa and the baby?" It was nearly midnight now. Dad had come to get us straightaway.

He smiled a fake smile. "I'm good. I'm fine. You should have called me."

"So Mom says."

He looked at Mom and Vivi. "This is Vivi," Mom said. "She's coming with us. We'd like to be back here tomorrow or the next day."

"I thought maybe you'd be ready to call it quits," Dad said. "You've got, how much, one week left?"

Mom said, "Four."

Dad said, "I want Dani to stay with me and Lisa while you're home."

"No way," I said.

"I want to make sure you're all right."

"I'd rather be burned in oil," I said. "I'd rather be set down naked and slathered with peanut butter in a field full of grizzly bears. I'd rather—"

"That's enough, Dani!" My mother's eyes flashed dangerously. To my father she said, "She's adjusting, she's eating plenty, the blisters just happened today—"

"You can't make me," I said.

Mom continued, almost pleading. "This has been good for her, for both of us." To me she said, "You'll stay with your father. Period. And you'll behave."

Which was how I found myself at two in the morning in a bed with pink sheets in my father's new house. You've maybe heard stories about people who sleep in the woods for so long that when they come back to civilization, real beds feel too soft, too uncomfortable. Wrong. I didn't like my dad and I really hated Lisa, but their guest bedroom was heaven on earth. No smells. No thru-hikers grunting. No mice. No insects.

Lisa, late the next morning, reminded me of a mother bear

out to defend her cubs. She curled her hand protectively over her little pregnant belly, and she looked at me only when she thought I wasn't looking at her. Dad served breakfast. Neither Lisa nor I spoke.

"How're your feet?" Dad asked. He had made me a bacon sandwich, my favorite thing on earth for breakfast, and gave me a cup of tea with the right amount of sugar already in it. I took a sip and discovered the sweetness, and tears came to my eyes.

"Fine," I said.

Dad sat down and looked at me earnestly. "Any signs of infection?"

Lisa toyed with her piece of toast. "I think—"

I cut her off. "There's no redness, there's no pus, the cracks are starting to make new skin. My boots fit. I've gotten a few blisters, but nothing like this so far. It was just because of Trailhead, because of pulling his pack downhill." I spoke quietly. Dad leaned forward, listening.

"Who's Trailhead?" he asked.

I explained about Trailhead and how he'd wrecked his knee. Dad grimaced. Lisa said, "He teaches high school English and he calls himself *Trailhead*?"

Dad took a sip of coffee. "It's a technical term," he said. "The trailhead is the start of the trail."

I could see Lisa hadn't known that. "Do you like to hike?" I asked her.

"I've never done it," she said.

"Well, Dad mostly likes to go alone," I said. "So I don't suppose you have to worry."

Lisa cleared her throat. "I'm glad you're finished. Your father has been worried sick."

He looked perfectly healthy to me. "I'm not done," I said.

"We're going back tomorrow." I looked at Dad, who nodded. He might be worried, but he was sticking with the plan.

"So long as you promise to call me whenever you can from now on," he said. "I want you to stay in touch."

"We aren't near phones very often," I said.

"I think this is ridiculous," Lisa said. She set her fork down on her plate, and it made a hard, angry *clink*. "Why you are giving your own child permission to keep doing this, I just don't understand. She's twelve years old! You don't ask her if she'd like to try a beer, do you? You don't ask her if she feels like smoking a cigarette! Why are you letting her skip school, grunge around in the woods, and hurt herself?" She put her hand to the little stupid swelling on her belly. She said, "When our baby is born, we're going to raise it *right*."

If I moved or spoke I would do something awful. I wanted to hurl plates at the wall, or smash Lisa's perfect nose into her petite bowl of non–puke-inducing cereal. I wanted to say something so mean she would never, ever, forget it. I figured I always had plenty of reason to hate Lisa, but until now I'd never realized that she hated me, too.

I said nothing, did nothing.

Dad said, very quietly, "Dani turned out all right. Though I'm not sure I can take the credit."

"Katahdin," I whispered. Dad nodded.

"You've got no right to criticize her," he continued in the same low voice, as though he were speaking a foreign language, as though the words were difficult to say. "You weren't in our house, you don't know what it was like. Katahdin is my responsibility, and her mother's. Not yours."

Lisa didn't back down. "I've got some say in this house, I hope. If she's going to stay here—"

I said, "I'm not going to stay here."

"You can stay here anytime you want," said Dad. "You can live here if you'd like to." He said it like he meant it. A look of utter horror crossed Lisa's face, just for a moment. I saw it, Dad saw it, and I saw him see it. "You are my child," he continued in a firmer tone. "You are my family. I will never forget that."

"Do you forget Springer?" I asked.

"Never," he said. "I never will."

Later Dad came into the guest room. I had taken a shower and changed into the cleanest of my clothes, and packed my gear and made the bed so that no one could tell I had been there. I bet Lisa would change the sheets anyhow, the moment I left.

"I'm sorry," Dad said. "She shouldn't have said those things. We all have to adapt. That includes Lisa, too. She's been under a lot of stress lately. It's a difficult time for her. She's worried about the baby."

"Duchenne muscular dystrophy is X-linked recessive," I said. "The baby can't get it from you."

"I think she's worried about other things," Dad said.

"Like what?"

Dad shook his head. "I don't know. All pregnant women worry about their babies. But anyway, I'm sorry you had to hear all that."

She should be the one apologizing, not him.

I tugged at the drawstring on my pack. "Can you take me home?"

I wanted him to say no, stay here for the day. We'll work it out. I'll make Lisa behave. I wanted him to say, *You're my daughter. You're important to me.* "Sure," he said. "You can tell Mom I'll take you all back to Erwin tonight if you want. I left the tax return on the counter with all her other mail: she'll just have to sign it."

He put his arm around my shoulder, a rare gesture. "I mean it about staying here. Anytime you want to, you can. We'll make it work out. I know it's been tough on you—but Lisa's a lovely person, she really is. You just need to get to know her."

Not in a hundred million years. I said, "I'll let you know."

At home Mom was sitting cross-legged on the carpet in the middle of Springer's bedroom. The air in the house was thick and choky; dust motes floated heavily in the air. Mom had her eyes shut. She looked like she was doing yoga. Mom never did yoga.

"Where's Vivi?" I asked.

"Bathtub," said Mom. "I think she's been in there for half an hour."

I walked in and sat down on the floor beside her. She opened one eye and studied me. "I think we should sell this house," she said.

"Why? We're coming back."

Mom shrugged. "Are we, really? To this house? I don't know. I don't think I want to. Maybe you've got good memories here. I don't. If you could live anywhere, where would it be?"

Here. Here in this house, eight years ago, Springer healthy, Mom happy, Dad laughing all the time. New flowered wallpaper in my bedroom—which got taken down when it became Springer's room, the only bedroom on the first floor, the only one a wheelchair could go into.

I lay down and put my head in my mother's lap. I wanted to say, Remember my flowered wallpaper? But I couldn't. "When we get back, I mean," Mom said. "When we're finished. Think about it. We don't have to stay here. We can go anywhere we want. Chicago. Wyoming. I could get a job somewhere interesting. Maybe I could even get an interesting job."

Dad doesn't live in Wyoming. I felt a stab of anger over Lisa and New Baby. Mom stroked my hair. "Where do you want to go?" she asked.

"Erwin."

"Mmmm," she said. "Good start."

April 12
Stan Murray Shelter (Tennessee)
Miles hiked today: 12
Total miles hiked on the Appalachian Trail: 371
Weather: sunny, warm

We were three days back on the Trail before Mom asked me, as we were boiling noodles in front of the shelter at night, "Did you talk to any of your friends when we were home?"

I took a deep breath. I knew this would come out sometime. "I don't have any friends."

Mom put down her spoon. She looked concerned. "Why not? What happened?"

"Nothing," I said.

"Why didn't you call Tanner?"

I didn't say anything.

"Honey?" Mom said. "Why didn't you call Jane?" She came over to me. "Did something happen?"

I looked at the ground. "When Springer died, Jane said she was sure I was sad but at least I wouldn't have to be embarrassed anymore." Once I got started the words tumbled over each other in a rush. "I got mad and said nothing was embarrassing about my brother, and she said, 'You know, the way his feet were and everything.' "

As he grew older Springer's feet curled down and in. They looked small and helpless; they reminded me of baby rabbits. It was a side effect of his MD. He couldn't wear shoes.

"And Tanner said . . . and Tanner said"—I had to stop and catch my breath, because Tanner had been my best friend— "she said, 'Jane doesn't get it, but she's kind of right anyway, isn't she? Now your mom can pay attention to you.'

"I was so angry, but I didn't know what to say to them, and after a while every time I was with them they were so careful not to talk about Springer that I hated it. And Jane started spending the night at Tanner's house, and I didn't want to be around them, I just didn't want to. And now the noodles are burning."

Mom jumped and grabbed the pot and turned off the stove. "This is why you started walking every day," she said.

I shrugged. "Not why, maybe, but when. I had to do something. I always felt better, walking. Can we talk about Springer sometimes? Nobody ever will."

"He's the elephant in our room," Mom said. She looked so sad that I hugged her.

"Why is he an elephant?" I asked.

She shook her head. "It was a poem I read once, about how when a person dies, no one will talk about them—if you loved the person that died, you feel like there's an elephant in the room but everyone is pretending it's not there. It takes up all the extra room and bumps into the furniture, and everyone just pretends it's not there."

"You didn't talk about him, either," I said.

"Oh, honey," she said. "I was thinking about him so much I

123

felt like I was talking about him all the time." She handed me a spoon. "Better eat while it's hot." I started eating.

Mom leaned back against a tree. "We'll talk about him, I promise. I'll tell you a good memory now. Okay?"

Vivi came back from the spring. It was slow-running even though the weather hadn't been especially dry. "We're telling good stories," Mom told her. "I'm telling about the day Springer was born." Vivi settled herself on the ground. Mom kept talking.

"It was late spring, a few days before he was due. I had had some pains the night before, and I'd even thought that maybe the baby was coming, but I wasn't sure, and it didn't hurt so badly that I couldn't sleep, so I went to sleep. Then I woke up at three A.M. and I knew I was really in labor.

"I started walking around the bedroom. Your dad and I had a tiny apartment then, just four small rooms. I walked to the end of the bed, turned around, and walked back. Your dad didn't wake up. Outside it was black dark, but when I stopped to open the window, a rush of air came into the room, and it smelled like pine trees and flowers. It smelled like spring had on the Appalachian Trail. We had only been off the Trail seven months and we talked about it all the time, so the smell seemed like a good omen for the day.

"After a bit your dad woke up. He watched the clock and helped me time a few contractions. He wanted to go to the hospital right away, but I said I wasn't ready. So then he said I shouldn't skip breakfast. He got out of bed and got dressed, and went into the kitchen and made pancakes."

"Pancakes?" I said. A faint memory came back—me standing beside Springer on a chair pulled close to the stove, the smell of bacon frying, the heat coming off the brown griddle. Daddy making pancakes, long ago.

"It was my favorite breakfast," Mom said. "Pancakes and a

124

pot of tea, and a plate of fresh sliced oranges. I ate for half an hour.

"Then we did go to the hospital. By then there were a few cars on the road, and the sky had that inky look it gets right before a clear dawn. I looked inside every car we passed, trying to get a glimpse of the people. I had this weird feeling that for all of them, for most of the people everywhere, that day was just another plain, ordinary, boring day.

"But for me it was the most astonishing day of my life. Springer was born by midafternoon. He had the most wide-open blue eyes and the darkest black hair. He didn't look like anyone I'd ever seen before. He was perfect."

Except for the fatal genetic flaw. "And you were happy," I said.

Mom paused and set her lips together. "Know what? I wasn't really. My mom and dad died when I was in college, you knew that. After I saw Springer all I could think of was them, and how happy they would have been, and how much I missed them. I was so happy to have Springer, but I felt sad."

"I'm never having children," I said.

"Well," she said.

"Also, I'm sorry, but I ate all the noodles. Even yours."

Mom shook her head and laughed in a tired way. "Go rinse the pan," she said. "I'll cook more."

"It wasn't an ordinary day for everybody, though," I said.

"What's that?"

"When you were looking in those cars. You didn't really know what was happening in people's lives. Maybe most of them were having an ordinary day, but some of them were having their best day ever."

"I suppose so," said Mom.

"And some of them," I said, "were having their worst."

April 14
Moreland Gap Shelter (Tennessee)
Miles hiked today: 15
Total miles hiked on the Appalachian Trail: 395
Weather: hotter than blazes   hot hot hot

We climbed the steps to the shelter and took our packs off inside. Mom threw herself onto one of the bunks. I bent to take off my boots. Sweat, sweat, nothing but sweat. Even in the shade of the woods, even high on the mountaintops, the sun was hot and the air thick and muggy. We'd had some warm days, but this was by far the hottest yet, and I'd been in a full-body sweat since nine A.M.

You wouldn't even think of the places you can sweat. In your ears, for one—not just trickling through your hair, but right down inside your ears. On the *tops* of your knees. And right down the middle of your backside, if you know what I mean. All day. I peeled my socks off. My feet felt pickled.

Mom heaved herself up. "I'm going to go soak my head," she said.

"Ugmph. Me too," said Vivi.

"I'll be right along," I said. "I'm going to change my shirt." I wanted to check out the register while they weren't around. I didn't know if Mom had ever realized there were messages for me. I wasn't going to tell her. Beagle was mine. Even with our quick trip home we were gaining on him; now we were only two days behind. I wondered if he knew how glad I was to read his messages. It was like he was walking with me. Every register, he was there.

I flipped back a page or two. Sure enough. *It's the same thing, day after day. Can't wait until Damascus. Good night, Katahdin, wherever you are.* I flipped to the end. *It's the same Trail, but always different. I love it. Katahdin.*

"What's in Damascus?" I asked Mom when she came back.

"Damascus?" she repeated, looking puzzled.

"People are writing about it in the register," I said. "They make it sound like something special."

"Oh, must be Trail Days. It's a big weekend festival. Damascus is a town in Virginia, we'll be there in a few days—"

"I know that," I cut in.

"But Trail Days isn't until the end of May, I think. I'm surprised they're talking about it in the registers already. A lot of thru-hikers go even if they have to hitch a ride to get there. We'll be off the Trail by then."

I hadn't been angry in days, really I hadn't. But something about the way she said it so casually, *We'll be off the Trail by then,* made me seethe. "Can we go?" I asked.

Mom said, "I really don't see the point. You going, Vivi?"

Vivi shook her head. "Not my scene. I'll be farther on, I'm not turning back for a party."

I scowled. "You never let me do anything I want," I said.

Mom sounded stern. "Such as hike right now? Don't be so dramatic. What would you do at Trail Days?"

"You didn't let me go to soccer camp last year." Sometimes

it seemed like all it would take was one little aggravation, and all the hurts from years ago would ooze right up and come out of my mouth. I sounded bratty even to myself, but I couldn't help it.

"That camp cost five hundred dollars—"

"Springer got to go to camp."

"Dani," she said. "What's gotten into you? Springer's camp was free, you know that." I did know it; it was sponsored by the Muscular Dystrophy Association, and it was only for kids with MD. Springer went every year from the time he was diagnosed. "Besides," she continued, angry herself now, "would you really have taken that week away from him? Or from us?"

It seemed like the only time I really realized how much work it was taking care of Springer, after he was stuck in a wheelchair, was when he was at camp and Mom and Dad didn't have to do it anymore. Bathing him, helping him use the toilet, and getting him dressed and undressed, into his chair and out of it. Dad did most of the personal stuff, after Springer got old enough to be embarrassed about Mom seeing him naked. Every morning and night, it took Dad nearly an hour. Even little things like going to the grocery store were easier without Springer. When he was at camp, the rest of us went out for ice cream in the evenings and went to movies without having to sit in the back where the wheelchairs fit. We were more relaxed.

Springer told me once that camp was the only place he felt normal—the one week every year when no one stared at him because he used a wheelchair, the one week he didn't have to explain his feet or his weakness to anyone. He got to go swimming in a lake at camp and play baseball, and one year he even got to ride a horse. Riding a horse felt like walking, he said. He could remember when his legs moved the same way.

So, no, I wouldn't have taken that week away, not from any of us.

"After he died, that was how I imagined our lives were going to be," I said. "Like when Springer was at camp."

"He's not at camp," Mom said.

"I know that." I picked at a scab on my leg. "Why didn't you ever let him come to my soccer games?"

Mom looked wary. "I let him," she said.

"No, you didn't!" I was angry again. "I always wanted him to come, I used to ask him and ask him, and he said you told him no. He said you wouldn't let him."

Mom sighed. "Should we just cook dinner and have a nice evening, or should we continue this conversation?"

"I'm not hungry," I said.

"Okay." She smoothed out her face. "Time to grow up a bit, then, and quit blaming me for everything. Springer didn't want to go to your games, Katahdin. He asked me not to make him, and I couldn't do it. Why would I have kept him away, unless he didn't want to?"

"You did," I sniffed. "He would have come for me."

"He was a thirteen-year-old boy in a wheelchair," Mom snapped. "He hated being stared at. And he loved soccer. You might not be able to remember, but he played Kindersoccer when he was four and five years old. He tried to play when he was six, and he couldn't do it anymore. He couldn't run."

When he was eight, he was in a wheelchair. I remembered that.

"It broke his heart," Mom said. "It broke mine. He couldn't stand to watch you play. But I let you play anyway. I never told you not to play; I never even suggested that you shouldn't.

"You can't make him into a saint just because he's dead," she continued. "He was a good kid and a tough kid and he loved you, and he never would have come to your soccer games. He cussed too much and he didn't always listen and he never was any good at math. He talked back. He was not perfect."

"Stop it," I said. "I don't want to talk. I want to eat dinner."

"You're the one who wants everything out in the open," Mom said. She looked plenty angry herself, now that she'd worked up steam. "Don't go blaming me for everything. And quit pretending your brother's watching out for you. Quit mooning over this Beagle."

"I'm not mooning! I'm not pretending!" I threw one of my hiking boots against the wall, and it fell to the floor in a cloud of dust. I threw the other one after it, and then I stomped off into the woods and sat by myself for a while. When I got back, Mom was still sitting in the shelter where I'd left her, and she hadn't started dinner. Vivi hadn't started cooking, either. She was sitting near Mom, equally silent and still.

I cooked, enough for us all.

Later, in the middle of the night, I remembered something. I got out of my tent and poked my head into hers. "I don't blame you for everything," I said aloud into the quiet darkness. "I don't blame you for Springer." She didn't reply.

April 19
Damascus, Virginia
Miles hiked today: 12
Total miles hiked on the Appalachian Trail: 454
Weather: clear

The next morning we were quiet and tense with each other. "We're going to walk hard today," Mom said. "We're going to *move*."

We were hiking along a ridgeline in woods. Vivi was up ahead, out of sight; Mom and I were close together. It was an ordinary day. "There are fewer of us now, have you noticed?" Mom said out of nowhere.

"Sure," I said, thinking she meant Springer.

She sighed. "Thru-hikers. There aren't so many now."

"Why not?"

"We've walked over four hundred miles. Lots of people don't make it this far. They've dropped out."

I thought about that as we started to descend. Nobody could blame Trailhead, say, for stopping, but I didn't know about the rest. If Mom would give me the chance, I'd be glad to keep going. "Think it's laziness?" I asked. We caught up with Vivi, who had stopped by a spring and was filtering water.

Mom splashed a tiny bit of water onto her hand and mopped her face with it. In the heat we didn't waste water; sources were few and far between, and some that were marked on our maps had dried up. "Laziness?" she asked. I nodded. "I don't think that's the right word," she said.

"Think of it this way," said Vivi. "If you've made a mistake, is it smarter to keep doing the wrong thing, or stop and do something different?"

Mom asked me, "Why did you want to hike the Appalachian Trail?"

"Me?"

"Yes, you."

"It's long," I said.

Vivi snorted. Mom waited.

"I wanted to get away from everything," I said. "But I wanted something to *do,* I wanted to be able to walk. And I wanted to be far away from people, but not too far so I could get food and everything. And I like mountains."

Mom took a sip of Vivi's filtered water. "That's a pretty good answer," she said after a pause. "You were wrong, of course, to run away. No matter what, you shouldn't have done that."

"I thought you'd never let me. I thought you wouldn't—"

"Well, you were wrong there, too. But at least your reasons for going were good. Though even a person who had a good reason might stop early."

"Maybe."

"The world's not black and white," she said.

"What were your reasons?" I asked.

She took another sip of water and looked away.

"I answered," I said, my voice rising. "You should, too. It's not fair—"

"The first time I hiked the Trail," Mom said, interrupting me, "it was because I didn't know what else to do." Vivi nodded as though she understood. I didn't. "My parents had died," Mom said, "and I was still adjusting to that. I graduated from college, but I didn't know what I was supposed to do next. I read a magazine article about the Appalachian Trail and I just hightailed it out here. It was early spring—I'd graduated early, winter term—and I was lonely and scared. That hike was a lot different from this one. I made friends at the shelters every night. I went into town with big groups of people. I spent four days at Damascus during Trail Days, having a big party. And I was falling in love with your father."

Mom smiled and shook her head. "Well. It was a lot more of a social thing for me then, that's all I'm saying. The Trail was the same, but I was different. I needed to figure out who I was."

"Did you?" I asked.

"Partially."

"Why are you hiking now?"

"To be with you."

I must have made a face, because she put out her hand and touched my arm. "I figured you might have a good reason," she said softly. "That was good enough for me."

That night it got hotter, not cooler. We lay on top of our sleeping bags, alone in the shelter. I wished we'd made better time. I wanted to catch up with Beagle.

On Wednesday we reached Damascus. I was pretty eager to see it, and Vivi said she was, too. We were going to take a zero day, do laundry and get supplies.

We hit an asphalt road and could walk three abreast. Mom said, "They call this the friendliest town on the Trail."

"Is this where you were married?" I asked.

133

"Why would you think that?"

"I thought that's what you said."

"No," Mom said. "That was Harpers Ferry. Another important Trail town."

"John Brown?" cut in Vivi. "Started the Civil War?"

"Really?" I said. "I thought it was just famous because of the Trail."

"Aren't you supposed to be homeschooling?" Vivi teased me.

"If Mom lets us keep going, I'll put an algebra book in my pack and do fifty problems every night," I promised. I looked at Mom. "But you did get married while you were thru-hiking?"

She shot me a look. "Of course."

"So you'd known Dad for . . ."

She sighed. "A little over two months. Not long enough, but there you are."

"Was it in a church?"

"Justice of the peace," Mom said. "The courthouse."

"That doesn't sound very romantic," I said.

"Oh, I don't know." She began to smile. "I bought a new white T-shirt to wear for the ceremony—actually three white T-shirts, they came three to a pack. And some new socks and new underwear. And I carried a bouquet of wildflowers that Juniper—she was a thru-hiker with us—picked from the side of the Trail, and Juniper and Wild Cat—he was best man—tied empty tin cans to our backpacks and a sign that said 'Just Married.' "

"Tin cans?" I wrinkled my nose.

"You know, like they hang on the backs of cars? When someone gets married, Dani, they hang tin cans off the back bumper of the car that the couple drives away in."

It was the first I'd heard of it. "What happened to Juniper and Wild Cat?" I asked.

"Juniper, I don't know, she started out in Colorado after the Trail. She was going to run an outfitter's or a hiking service or something, be a ski instructor in the wintertime. I heard from her for a few years afterward. Wild Cat twisted his knee in the Whites and left the Trail; we didn't hear from him again."

"Like Trailhead," I said.

"Yep. Bad hiker injury. But this was back before e-mail, remember—you had to write to people, or call them. It was harder to keep in touch."

I knew the Whites meant the White Mountains in New Hampshire. You hike above the tree line there, where the Trail is nothing but rocks. "Are the Whites hard?"

Mom shrugged. "Sure. But they're also eleven hundred miles away. We don't need to worry about them. Where should we stay tonight? What looks good?"

"A nice bed-and-breakfast with a good dining room," suggested Vivi.

"A hostel," I said.

"Maybe a happy compromise—" said Mom.

Up ahead I saw someone on the sidewalk—someone tall and thin and familiar. *"Beagle!"* I shouted, and ran.

April 21
Deep Gap (Virginia)
Miles hiked today: 16
Total miles hiked on the Appalachian Trail: 481
Weather: hot, humid, horrible

I hate everything. I cannot believe I am still hiking. The worst part: Mom is making me. "I want to quit," I said this morning.

"Not today," she answered.

"You said we could quit anytime I wanted. So now I want to quit." I'd been up half the night crying into Springer's old shirt. "I'm tired of being out here. Nothing changes. I want to go home."

Mom looked me up and down with a cool expression on her face and said, "No."

"What do you mean, no?"

"We're hiking, Dani. A quick grocery run and that's it. Get your boots on."

So we hiked. Mom went ahead with Vivi. They waited for me every mile or so. I walked slowly when I was walking and I sat when I wanted to sit and I cried a lot of the time. We still made sixteen miles. I feel like some kind of horrible robot walking machine.

I couldn't believe what had happened in Damascus.

The first thing was, Beagle didn't recognize me. I rushed up to him and threw my arms around him, and he went all stiff and pushed me away the way you would if some complete stranger tackled you in the street. "Whoa!" he said.

"Beagle," I said. "Beagle, it's me."

He looked at me hard. The two people with him looked at me, too.

"Katahdin," I said, my voice fading a little. "You write me notes in the registers."

"I'm sorry," he said. He looked bewildered, embarrassed, alarmed. "I don't know what notes you mean."

"Good night, Katahdin, wherever you are!"

He looked away again, his face turning red. The two guys he was with stared at me. "Oh, right," he said at last. "You're the kid from the first day. Sure, I remember. But I didn't think you were hiking anymore. Man, I would not have recognized you, either, if you hadn't said something. You must have gotten taller, or—what'd you do, cut your hair?"

I hadn't done anything to my hair. Beagle looked different, too, skinnier and dirtier, but I had recognized him. "You write me notes," I repeated.

He shook his head. He was smiling but the smile didn't seem directed at me, not in any personal way. "Man, I just didn't recognize you," he said. "I really never expected to see you again. I'm sorry."

I could tell he expected me to say, "That's okay," or "No problem," or something like that. "Come meet my mom again," I said. "And Vivi. Come have dinner with us."

He looked at his watch. "We're in kind of a hurry."

"Well. Okay. See you at the shelters, then."

He shook his head. "We're headed for the bus station," he said. "We're out of here."

"For how long?" I asked. I felt like my feet had grown into the sidewalk, like I couldn't have moved if I'd tried.

"For good," he said. He sighed. "See, all along, my favorite part of the Trail has been the town stops. And this week I realized, I like being at home better than I like hanging out in some strange Trail town. This was an excellent idea—an excellent *idea,* but I am completely done." He grinned at the guys with him. "I guess some people just aren't meant to be thru-hikers."

"Oh." I couldn't think of anything to say.

"So, see you. Or, no, I guess I won't. Good luck, then. Like, good luck with whatever."

He turned and started walking, and his two friends walked with him. "Who was that?" one of them asked, his voice floating back to me. "Your girlfriend? She looks pretty young." He laughed.

"Just some kid," Beagle answered. "I bought her breakfast back at Springer. She looked scared to death. She calls herself Katahdin—I can't remember her real name."

Like, good luck with whatever. She calls herself Katahdin—I can't remember her real name.

I was not scared to death. I was never scared to death. Beagle looked back over his shoulder. He gave me a half-smile that might have been an apology. His other buddy said, "You wrote her *notes*?" Beagle turned away and kept walking. He left me alone.

That night Mom and Vivi and I ended up going to a pizza place for dinner. I could not stop crying, and I begged Mom to take me home. Vivi and Mom kept looking at each other, and nodding, and ignoring my tears. When the waitress asked, "Hey, is she okay?" Vivi said, "No, but she's getting there."

Now it was two days later, and I was still on the Trail, where I didn't want to be, while Beagle was home, wherever his home was. Mom and Vivi had stopped at Deep Gap and set up camp, and since they got there first I had to stop, too. I wished I could get away from them. If I couldn't go home, I wanted to be alone.

Mom went for water. Vivi came and sat next to me. I had taken off my pack and gotten Springer's shirt out and was just sitting still, holding it. Vivi gave me a sympathetic look. "Go ahead and cry," she said.

"I've been crying for two days!" I wailed. I wiped my eyes. "I just can't believe Beagle left," I said. "I can't believe he's gone."

Vivi didn't say anything. She handed me her water bottle and I took a gulp and wiped at my eyes.

"Why did he just leave?" I said. Tears kept coming like they were never going to stop. I looked up and saw Mom coming back, coming toward us. "Why would he do that?" I said. "Why did he have to go and *die*?"

I took a huge breath of air in a shuddering gulp and my shoulders started to shake. Vivi put her arms around me, and then Mom did, too. Shiny tear tracks ran down Mom's cheeks, and tears dripped from her chin. "I don't know," Mom said. "I just can't understand it, either."

"I miss him," I said. "He was not supposed to die."

"I know, honey, I know," she said.

Vivi patted me. "I'm sorry," I said to her.

"Blessed almighty," Vivi drawled, "I've been sad some, too."

Eventually night fell. The stars came out and the air smelled strong and sweet. We made dinner and ate it, but we didn't clean it up. We just sat, quietly, and sometimes Mom and I cried. "He really was not supposed to die," Mom said softly. Vivi shifted her weight and turned her head, listening.

"He had a life expectancy of about twenty years," Mom continued. "He was only thirteen. Duchenne kids—always boys, it's genetic and linked that way—start off seemingly normal, but their muscles get progressively weaker over time. They die when their hearts are too weak to pump blood, or their diaphragms too weak to let them breathe."

"Or both," I said.

Mom nodded. "Or both. Springer was in good shape—"

"And then he got pneumonia," I said. "He was in the hospital, but he was doing well. We all thought he was fine. I went to see him after school, and I told him I'd bring his homework in so he wouldn't get too far behind."

"I told him I loved him, but I didn't stay the night," Mom whispered. I found her hand in the darkness and squeezed it hard. "I wasn't with him when he died. The nurses checked him through the night. At one check he was asleep, and at the next he was dead, and no one was with him when it happened."

"And so here we are," she said. "Taking a little walk. Katahdin and I." She got up and picked up the supper pot.

I thought Vivi was going to think we were completely nuts, but all she said was, "There you are, then."

"There you have it," Mom replied.

April 28
Post Office, Bland, Virginia
Miles hiked today: 7
Total miles hiked on the Appalachian Trail: 585
Weather: rain

I woke up at Deep Gap still sad enough to cry. I didn't think I'd felt that sad since the morning Mom sat on the edge of my bed and told me Springer was dead. I didn't think I'd ever felt that sad. I lay on my back and let tears roll through my hair.

After a while I got up and went out to find Mom.

"Have you ever been this sad?" I asked her.

"I don't know," she said. "Some days." She lit the stove and put a pan of water on to boil. "You can quit the Trail now if you want to," she said. "You can quit today, or we can go on."

"Until when?" I asked.

"You know the answer to that. We've got another ten days."

I didn't say anything until we'd finished breakfast. I'd stopped crying by then. I said, "I say we go on."

She smiled. "I figured you would."

The mountains of Virginia were pretty, covered in full green leaves. Between Deep Gap and Sugar Grove, a town where we stopped to buy groceries and do laundry, it was thirty-eight miles, and we covered it in less than two and a half days.

I was still sad part of every day, but for the first time it seemed okay to be sad. I didn't know why it hadn't before. As usual, Mom never seemed especially sad or especially happy. She did talk more, to me and to other hikers we met along the way, and not just about Springer, either. She started naming wildflowers for me, and pointing out different varieties of trees and birds, and kinds of rocks and other things I hadn't known she knew. We sat around after dinner talking with the other hikers besides Vivi, and it didn't feel strange. The day after Sugar Grove a whole group of us accepted an invitation to stay in someone's cabin for the night. I wouldn't have felt safe doing that if Mom and I were alone, but with five other hikers, three of them big, stinky guys, it was fine.

From Sugar Grove to Bland, Virginia, was fifty-six miles. Four days. Mom said it would be our last resupply. "Don't make faces at me, Katahdin," she said. "I can't help it. Our grand adventure is coming to an end."

Bland was not the place to end it. Bland was bland. We stood outside the post office. "Can I call Dad?"

"Of course," Mom said. "You can always call Dad."

Lisa answered. "It's Dani," I said. "Can I talk to Dad?"

"He's not here," she said. "How are you?"

"Fine."

"How's the hike?"

"Fine."

"When are you coming home?"

"Mom says next week."

"Well." She paused. I could imagine her on the other end

of the phone, rolling her eyes at how hard it was to pretend she liked me. "We've got good news. You've got a—" She cut herself off in midsentence.

"A what?" I asked.

"The baby's a boy," she said. "We just found out."

You've got a brother. That's what she had been going to say. I couldn't decide if I hated her more or less for not saying it.

I had a brother.

"We've picked out a name," Lisa said. "David. David Harper Brown."

"David *Harper* Brown?"

"That's right. Do you like it?"

"It's okay."

Lisa didn't say anything else for a moment. Neither did I. "I'll tell your dad you called. He'll be sorry he missed you."

"Okay," I said.

"You're sure you're okay? Nothing's wrong?"

"Nothing's wrong."

I hung up the phone and stared at it. David Harper Brown. Harper as in Harpers Ferry, I was sure of it. Not a mountain, but the midpoint. Another child named after the Trail.

"Do you like Lisa?" I asked Mom later. We were doing laundry at a motel that would let us use their machines even though we weren't going to stay there. Vivi had put her laundry in and left for the grocery, so I had a chance to talk to Mom alone.

"Lisa? Mmmm, no. Not really. Not at all, actually. It's kind of an odd question, wouldn't you say?" I told her about the baby's name. Mom nodded, then went back to the book she was reading—a dilapidated paperback someone had left in the laundry room.

"Don't you care?" I asked.

"Don't judge me, Katahdin," she said, sounding bored.

"But every time I'm around Lisa, I get the feeling she wishes I didn't exist."

"Well." Mom didn't say anything else for a few moments. "I don't know. People are complicated. How you feel about her, and how she feels about you, isn't set in stone. It can change."

"Do you wish she didn't exist?" I asked.

Mom grinned. "I won't say."

"If she didn't exist, would you still be married to Dad?"

Her grin faded. "I don't think so. I can't imagine that we would be. Our divorce was not her fault."

"If Springer hadn't died—"

Mom interrupted. "We talked about that once before. You're going to have to let it be. When you're older, I think you'll forgive us. Maybe not until then."

"If Springer had never been born—"

"Then what?" she asked.

I shook my head. I wasn't sure how to end the sentence, wasn't sure what I was trying to say. "I can't imagine it," I said.

"No," said Mom. "Nor can I."

May 1
Pine Swamp Branch Shelter (Virginia)
Miles hiked today: 20!
Total miles hiked on Appalachian Trail: 637
Weather: clear, cool evening

We were flying down the Trail, just flying. Twenty miles in a single day, nearly full packs, good weather. At lunch I brought up leaving the Trail, or rather, not leaving it. "You could get another month's sabbatical," I said.

"Theoretically, maybe," Mom said. "Practically, I think it would be more than my supervisor could take."

"But if you don't like your job anyhow—"

"I'd still rather keep it until I found a new one."

"But—"

"No buts, Dani."

Vivi squeezed my hand sympathetically, and later, when we had stopped and were waiting for my mom, she said, "I know you want to keep on, but you'll have time to come back when you're older."

"People always say that," I said. "It's complete garbage. You know it is. You told me all about your cancer and how you were treasuring every moment."

"Well, right. I mean, yes, you're correct, but you're also not old enough to make your own decisions. In a few years you will be, and statistically speaking you should still be alive at that time."

"Hah." We could see Mom now, making her way toward us. "Would you keep going, if you were in Mom's place?"

Vivi's face grew sad and thoughtful. "Honey, my kids are grown up and healthy. I can't even imagine your mom's place." She thought a moment longer and added, "You started out without her. Would you keep going without her, if you could?"

I thought about my first night on Springer Mountain, and all the nights since then. I shook my head. "No."

"Might want to tell her," Vivi said as Mom came within hearing range.

"Tell her what?" Mom asked.

I shrugged. "I'm glad you're here with me. I wouldn't have been able to do it alone. I wouldn't have wanted to, either."

"Thank you," Mom said.

At the end of the day, twenty miles from breakfast, we were all walking together in a row. Vivi led. She made a snorting sound about thirty yards from the shelter. "Hmph," she said, pointing. "Teenagers."

"I'm practically a teenager," I said.

"Oh, honey, you don't count. They've probably got boom boxes and beer."

Mom grinned. "If they've got beer, I'm going to make them share it."

They did not have beer, or boom boxes, or even CD players that I could tell. Their names were Flip, Jake, and Andrew. They had external-frame packs and well-worn boots, and they looked cool to me.

I couldn't tell you how I looked to them. It was hard to say which smelled worse, me or my pack, even though we'd done laundry in Bland only three days ago and so my clothes were cleaner than usual. You wouldn't believe how much you sweat, hiking in hot weather.

Vivi said, "Any bunks left for us?" We could see their gear lined up along the front of the shelter.

The one I later learned was named Jake said, respectfully, "No bunks, ma'am, there's just a floor in this shelter."

Vivi grinned. "Any floor left?"

"Yes, ma'am." He moved their stuff to one side a little and let us climb in. There was plenty of room. Andrew, who was a little kid only eight or nine years old, looked at us with wide eyes. He had black hair falling low over his forehead. "Are you thru-hikers?" he asked in a whisper.

"Vivi is," I told him. "Mom and I are doing the first seven hundred miles."

Some people have never heard of thru-hikers, some think it's weird ("Why would you want to do that?"), and some think it's very impressive and want to ask questions for half an hour. Flip, Jake, and Andrew were none of those. Flip said, "See, bud, told you we'd meet a thru-hiker," and Andrew said, "Wow," and Jake said, "We can show you where the water is— you went over the creek, but it's better if you go downstream a bit." In the end it was Flip who helped me carry the water bags and the filter.

He was tall and stringy-looking. The muscles on his calves stood out like he hiked all the time. He said, "I didn't know anybody my age thru-hiked."

"Section-hiked," I corrected him. "I want to go all the way, but we can't."

"Section-hiked that far," he said. "Pretty long section."

"I haven't seen anybody else our age, except weekend hikers," I said. "Nobody really serious. I'm sure I'm not the first, though."

"I heard once about a five-year-old boy," Flip said. "I figured he must be a rumor."

"Mom says someone told her his name once, so she thinks he might be for real." We reached the water, which was really running low, and I started to filter some.

"You heard about the blind guy?" Flip said.

"Everybody's heard about the blind guy," I said. He started his thru-hike with only his Seeing Eye dog as a guide. The dog was named Orient, and the blind guy called himself the Orient Express. They made it all the way.

"Andrew's my brother," Flip told me. "Jake and I come up here a couple times a year. We kept telling him he could come with us sometime."

Here is a list of questions Flip could have asked: Do you have brothers and sisters? (Did I? With Springer dead? Did David count?) How old are you anyhow? (He was fourteen, I would have guessed; I thought he looked older than me, but I still didn't know how I looked to him.) So where's your dad? How come your mom doesn't have a job?

Here is what he asked me: "Hiking that long, does it get lonely?"

"Yes and no," I said.

He picked up one of the water bags. "I always thought," he said, "that it would be a good kind of lonely."

We made a small campfire, the first I'd been near in several weeks, and we roasted hot dogs over the fire. They were Flip, Jake, and Andrew's hot dogs, but after they saw us watching them, they offered to share. They had plenty anyhow. Andrew looked amazed when I ate six. "Food is fuel," I told him. "I'm burning lots of fuel."

"Want another?" he asked.

"No, thank you."

"Good," he said.

Andrew fell asleep first, worn out from the hike, I guess, and then Mom and Vivi. Flip and Jake and I stayed around the fire, tossing small logs onto it and watching them fall into embers. They told me all about Pearisburg, West Virginia, where they lived, and about all the places they'd hiked nearby. I told them my favorite Trail stories. The night got cold, the wind sweeping down the mountain, and we built the fire higher. I got my long underwear top out of my pack and put it on. "It was snowing in North Carolina," I said. "It was frightening."

Flip looked at me over the edge of the fire. "Man, you get to wake up and hike every day!" he said. "That would be so cool. I wish I had your life."

I don't think he really meant it. But I let it be, all the same.

In the morning Mom and Vivi and I woke early, like we always did. Early mornings are the best times to hike. We moved around quietly so as not to wake the boys. I thought I saw Flip's eyes open as we walked away, but I couldn't be sure.

May 3
Near Niday Shelter (Virginia)
Miles hiked today: 12
Total miles hiked on the Appalachian Trail: 667
Weather: cooler, clear and sunny

Vivi left us that day.

She had been in a strange mood all morning. She had been walking fast, and waiting when we caught up, with an uncharacteristically impatient look on her face. At lunch she didn't want to rest, she wanted to keep going. Mom, on the other hand, wanted a nap. They stood facing each other and spoke like they were bad actresses in a play, reciting lines they didn't mean.

"No, if you're tired, we should rest."

"No, if you'd like to keep going, I'm fine."

They were both very polite and fairly cross. In the end we rested for half as long as Mom wanted, which meant they were both unhappy.

I wanted to keep walking, to tell the truth, but Mom looked so worn out that I didn't say so. At three-thirty P.M. we reached Laurel Creek Shelter. We'd made astonishing time. "Early night tonight," Mom said, unclipping her pack.

Vivi, our friend, looked so unhappy.

"What's wrong?" Mom asked her.

"I want to stay with you guys so much," she said. "But at the same time I want to keep hiking so much. I feel so strong now, I could easily go another five miles tonight." She paused. "Anyway, I can't decide whether I should stay with you all the way to the end. Maybe you need a little time on your own."

Mom said. "You can be with us. You're like our family. But you don't have to stay. You're going to need to find some new hiking partners anyhow. We won't be hurt if you start looking now."

Yes, we will, I thought. I saw the concern on Mom's and Vivi's faces. I saw how much they loved each other. All in that instant I realized that my mother would not be talked into continuing, tonight or later on. In three days we were leaving the Trail.

I held out my hand to Vivi. She took it and squeezed it. "I'll walk with you a little farther on," I said.

"Okay," Vivi said. "That would be good."

We walked another half mile. I'd left my pack at the shelter, so I could go along easily. "Good luck," I said when I was ready to turn back.

"You too," she said. She hugged me, quick and hard. "I'll keep in touch. You keep in touch, too."

The next morning Mom and I climbed Sinking Creek Mountain. Mom seemed to be sinking with every step. She simply could not hike fast, and she was crabby, too.

"Sinking Creek Mountain is part of the Eastern Continental Divide," I told her. I'd read it in the guidebook. "Water on one side of this mountain flows to the Mississippi, and on the other, to the Atlantic Ocean."

"Thank you, Ms. Park Ranger," Mom said. "I understand the concept of a continental divide. I'm also tired, and I have to climb another mountain before I can have dinner."

"No, you don't," I said. "We can stop before then."

"We were going to get to Pickle Branch."

"We can stop right *here.*"

She looked around, then said petulantly, "No, we can't. It's not a good place. And I want a pizza."

"Mom," I said, "have you got a bug in your eye?"

She looked at me in startled astonishment, and then we both burst out laughing. "Got a bug in your eye" was something from my childhood, something Mom used to say whenever Springer or I was whining, to make us laugh and get us over it.

"Where did that come from anyway?" I asked her. "Did you make it up?"

Mom shook her head. "You said it first. We were on a car trip—we were on vacation, this was before the MD—and you were worn out and started crying. You tried to get out of your car seat. When that didn't work, you yelled, 'I'm hot, I'm tired, I'm *bored,* and I've got a bug in my eye.' Springer thought that was hilarious. He wouldn't let us forget it. The whole rest of the trip, he kept asking you—"

"I remember," I said. " 'Dani, have you got a bug in your eye?' "

Mom grinned. "Right."

"Anyway," I said, "we can stop early for the night."

She made a face. "Don't you feel like we should keep going?"

"Not if you're tired."

"I don't know if I'm tired. We'll have a long day tomorrow if we stop now."

"Let's stop," I said.

It turned out to be an important afternoon. The air near our campsite was just perfect, warm in the sun with a fresh piney smell. We had a clear-running stream and a view of the mountains. I filtered water and set up our tents, then pulled some of our grubbier clothing out of our packs and washed it in the stream with the Dr. Bronner's soap that doesn't hurt the fishies. I figured we had enough time so that the clothes could dry in the sun.

Mom made tea and sat and watched me. "Feel better?" I asked.

"I do." She smiled. "But I miss Vivi. And I wish I had a newspaper. Or a book. Something."

"Too much nature?"

"No. But I'm used to newspapers. We'll be home in a few days. We'll have to get you signed up for summer school."

"It'll work out," I said.

"Do you feel like you'll just fit right back into your old life?" Mom asked.

I was wringing out a T-shirt. I spread it onto a bush before I answered. "I didn't fit into it when I left," I said. "That was part of leaving. I think I'll fit into something now. I could call Tanner, maybe. If she wants to be friends again I guess maybe I could be, too. Or I can find some new friends, probably. I guess I haven't thought about it."

"What have you thought about?"

I looked at the trees and stream. "I can't remember."

"I don't know what I'll do," Mom said. "This whole time we've been out here I haven't been able to think of a single thing I'd like to do when I get home."

"I thought you wanted to get a pizza," I said. She laughed and threw a handful of grass at me.

"It's been a treat, getting to hike the Trail a second time, and with you."

I thought of the blisters and mud and bugs and days of nothing but noodles for dinner.

"Maybe someday you'll get to do it again with your daughter," she said.

Oh, that hurt so much. "I'm never having children," I said. "Don't you understand?"

Her face closed up. "I don't think your childhood has been that horrible," she said. "We always did our best."

"But I don't want to have a baby like Springer," I said. "I don't think I could stand it. I wish I could, but I really can't."

Water from the wet shirt dripped onto my feet. Mom stood still, staring at me. She looked shocked. "Oh, honey," she said. She sprang up and wrapped her arms around me, cradling me tight against her chest. "Oh, honey, I didn't know you were worried about that. I'm so sorry. I'm so sorry."

"The minute they said Duchenne's, I'd know what was going to happen," I sobbed. "And even before then, I'd know what might happen. I'd be so scared. I'd know all along how much it was going to hurt."

Mom wiped the tears off my face with her shirttail. She rocked me back and forth. I saw that she was crying, too. "Katahdin, baby, you're fine," she said. "Listen. You're fine. You don't carry the Duchenne gene. You're going to have healthy babies. Don't you remember?"

I felt like someone had just poured ice-cold water down my back. Goose bumps rose up on my arms. "Remember what?"

"We had you tested, to see if you were a carrier."

I understood how the genetics worked. Mom had a bad gene, so there was a fifty-fifty chance that every boy she had would have Duchenne's, and die, and a fifty-fifty chance that every girl she had, including me, would have the bad gene and pass it on to her kids. Flip a coin—tails, you lose. I didn't remember a test. I didn't know there was a test.

"I guess you weren't old enough to understand," Mom said. "I thought you were. We told you all about it when we had it done—we had to. And we wanted you tested early because we thought you needed to know, growing up. We thought you did know."

"You never said—"

"We did say. I promise you." She wiped my face. "Oh, honey, we did. I didn't realize you didn't understand. I guess we all put it out of our minds since we knew we didn't have to worry. I'm so sorry you were worried still."

Healthy babies. No more dying. A girl to hike with me someday—or even a boy. A whole future without any more Duchenne's. "Did Springer know?" I asked.

"We told him when we told you," she said.

"Then he knew," I said. Springer never forgot anything.

"I'm sorry," Mom said again.

"It's okay," I said.

My whole future would change now: everything I thought, everything I knew. I looked up, expecting to see a hawk or an eagle or something soaring in the wind, like my hopes were soaring, like my happiness. The clear blue sky was empty. I listened to the creek splashing its way over rocks, I felt the sun hot on my cheeks. Everything seemed new, and I was filled with joy.

May 5
Catawba, Virginia
Miles hiked today: 6
Total miles hiked on the Appalachian Trail: 689
Weather: cooler, chance of rain

When you hike the Appalachian Trail, you get used to waking up and walking, waking up and walking, every day. You get used to feeling sore all the time in different parts of your body; you get used to being sweaty and dirty. You get wet when it rains. You sweat when it doesn't. You eat everything you can, every chance you get, and you realize that your body is a wonderful, powerful machine. If you stay on the Trail, you become amazed by what you can do.

When I started out in Georgia, it was as if I couldn't even see—I never really paid attention to the trees or the woods, or anything except the hard-packed path in front of me. Spring came, and I barely noticed. By the time Mom and I left the Trail at Catawba, Virginia, on the fifth of May, I felt like the beauty of the mountains and the woods was soaking into my bones. I noticed everything.

I woke up, somewhere along the Trail.

The last day, Mom said, "Maybe I'll take a test. They must have aptitude tests, don't you think? Like in high school?"

"I haven't been to high school yet, Mom."

She ignored that. "There are tests you take, they tell you what you'd be good at, like a scientist or, I don't know, a plumber, or something."

"What did yours say in high school?"

"I can't remember. It wasn't very interesting."

"Maybe the tests are better now," I said.

"Yeah. Well, that's what I'm hoping." She looked pretty cheerful about it. "What do you want?"

Suddenly I knew one thing. "I don't mind if we sell our house, but I don't want to move to a new town."

Mom nodded. "Because you don't want to change schools?" she asked.

"I don't know," I said. "I mean, I guess I don't, but that's not the reason."

She waited for the reason.

"I don't want to be away from Dad," I said. "I think he does want to be around me, but Lisa will make it harder, and if we moved that would make it a lot harder, too. And I think I'd like to get to know David Harper as he grows up, and that'll be tough if I'm not close by."

"Okay," Mom said. "We'll stay in town. I'd like to sell the house, though. I'm thinking an apartment would be less work."

"I'll do the work," I said. "I'll help. I won't mind."

"You don't want an apartment?"

"I want trees."

"Okay," she said. "As long as you promise to help."

———

Our last day was six miles, a stroll. We took it easy, stopped for lunch. "What happens now?" I asked. "Can we take a bus home from Catawba?"

Mom shook her head. "I doubt it. They've got a restaurant and a motel. I thought we'd call Nancy and see if she'll come get us tomorrow. It wouldn't take her more than four or five hours."

"Okay."

"I'm proud of you, of the way you're handling this now. I know you'd like to keep going."

We'd completed one third of the Appalachian Trail. I knew so much more about hiking than when I'd started out; I knew for sure now that I could make it to Katahdin, if only I had the chance. I guessed I knew one answer to why some people quit the Trail: because they didn't have a choice.

"I've been thinking," Mom went on. "Whatever job I end up with, they'll have to give me some kind of vacation time. So we could take a week or two every year and come back to the Trail. We could keep heading north. It still counts as a thru-hike, you know, if you finish the whole thing in sections."

A hundred miles in a week, if we were fast. Maybe ten years to finish, depending on how many weeks Mom could take. "I'd like that," I said.

We came to the state highway and walked along it west toward Catawba. I saw the store first, and then the flag flying by the post office. I saw a familiar car parked in front of the store. Then I saw my father.

"Dad!" I called. *"Dad!"*

He walked toward us. "Need a lift home?"

"How did you know? How did you know where we were?"

"Lisa told me you were in Bland," he said. "I just figured you'd be here about now."

Mom laughed. "How many days have you been waiting for us?"

Dad checked his watch. "A few hours. I swear. No more." He gave me a kiss as I got in the car. "I know a great restaurant on the way home. I'll treat you both to dinner."

"Where's Lisa?" I asked.

"Home. Maybe you could stop by and say hi to her tomorrow."

"Maybe," I said.

September 26
114 Clear Mountain Road, Bristol, Tennessee
Miles hiked today: 0
Total miles hiked on the Appalachian Trail:
695 and holding
Weather: sunny and warm

I was named after Katahdin, a mountain in Maine. My brother Springer was named for a mountain in Georgia. The Appalachian Trail stretched between us, over two thousand miles long, and I think that when I set out to thru-hike it I hoped I might find Springer at the end. That's how much I missed him, how much I still miss him sometimes.

For now, though, I am one of the nine out of ten: one of the ones that quit. When Mom and I got home after our time on the Trail, we sold our house and moved to a cabin on the ridgeline of a knob. It is not perfect. The rooms are small, the bathtub leaks, and mice are invading the kitchen. But it is perfect for us. Trees surround us and we feel close to the sky. The road is so narrow and winding that the school bus can't get up and down, so it picks me up and drops me off at an intersection near the bottom. This means I get to climb up and down a very small mountain every day.

I spent the summer taking classes and studying; in the end

I was allowed to stay with my class. On the last Saturday of July, Mom and I drove to Nantahala and went white-water rafting. I won't say it wasn't fun. Then on August first, eleven months to the day after my brother Springer died, my brother David Harper was born.

When I got to the hospital his little bassinet had been wheeled into my stepmother's room. I hesitated just inside the door. Dad looked up, smiling. Lisa held David Harper, her arms curving around him like she meant to shield him forever from all the dangers in the world. But when I sat down on the edge of the chair by her bed, she set him in my arms.

He was so small and beautiful. He took my breath away.

Lisa cleared her throat. "When he's a little older," she said, "would you consider baby-sitting once in a while?"

"Well," I said. "Okay." I touched his tiny finger, soft as a kitten's paw.

Lisa said, "I know we could depend on you."

I still don't like her, don't get me wrong. But I don't hate her quite so much.

The first anniversary of Springer's death came and went. I remembered how I'd planned to spend it on the top of Mount Katahdin. I felt like I'd failed him, even though I knew I'd done the best I could.

The letter came the fourth week of September. It was a bright, clear day, of the sort that always reminded me of our best days on the Trail. When I climbed up the road after school, I took the mail out of our mailbox and thumbed through it as I walked toward the house.

"Susan and Katahdin," the envelope said. No last names. It had been forwarded from our old house. I didn't recognize the handwriting, but still a thrill traveled slowly up my spine. I stopped and carefully slit the envelope open. I shook it, and a photograph fell into my hand.

It was Vivi. She was standing next to the sign that marked the northern end of the Appalachian Trail. She looked thin, and tired, and radiantly happy.

A wave of pride and longing swept over me. I closed my eyes, and for a moment I could feel myself standing where she stood, rocks under my feet, cold wind hard against me. *Oh, Vivi,* I thought. *Oh, Springer.*

There was a letter in the envelope, too. I unfolded it and began to read it as I walked quickly toward the house. I couldn't wait to tell my mother. Vivi had made it to Katahdin.

Someday I would, too.

AFTERWORD

A man named Benton McKaye came up with the idea for the Appalachian Trail. He later said that he first thought of creating a hiking trail along the ridgelines of the Appalachian Mountains, from Georgia to Maine, in 1905, but it was an article he wrote in 1921 describing his idea that really sparked public imagination. At the time many parts of the proposed Trail, especially in Maine and southwest Virginia, were absolute wildernesses—and yet construction of the Trail began the next year. The entire length was opened in 1936. Some sections have been changed from time to time, but the basic Trail has remained the same. It now stretches 2,167 miles from the top of Springer Mountain, in Georgia, to the top of Mount Katahdin, in Maine, all on protected land.

Early Trail planners did not believe thru-hikes were possible or even desirable. In 1948, the first man to thru-hike, Earl Shaffer, had to show Trail officials his photographs and diary entries from all along the Trail before they believed he'd done what he said. But soon more and more people were attempting to thru-hike. The first woman to do so was Emma Gatewood (folks called her Grandma). She finished her first thru-hike in 1955, at age sixty-seven, and went on to complete a second thru-hike and section-hike a third.

Supreme Court Justice William O. Douglas also completed a thru-hike in sections. A six-year-old boy named Michael Cogswell, traveling with his parents, took eight months to complete a thru-hike in 1980 (the youngest female thru-hiker on record was eleven years old). In 1990, a blind man named Bill Irwin successfully thru-hiked with his guide dog, Orient. Bill's Trail name was Orient Express. Dan "Wingfoot" Bruce, now head of the Center for Appalachian Trail Studies, has thru-hiked seven times.

The Appalachian Trail Conference, which oversees the local hiking clubs and volunteers that maintain the Appalachian Trail, has its headquarters at the midpoint of the A.T., in Harpers Ferry, West Virginia. The Center for Appalachian Trail Studies is in Hot Springs, North Carolina. Both organizations offer lots of information to anyone who wants to learn more about the Trail.

Hikers say, "Hike your own hike." The Appalachian Trail is different for each person who comes to it. I have tried to make Dani's and her mother's hike as real and accurate as possible. Any errors are entirely my own.

ABOUT THE AUTHOR

Kimberly Brubaker Bradley was born in Fort Wayne, Indiana. After earning her bachelor's degree from Smith College, she worked as a research chemist, then became a freelance writer. Her first novel, *Ruthie's Gift,* won her a *Publishers Weekly* "Flying Start" honor. Her most recent novel, *Weaver's Daughter,* was a Bank Street College Children's Book of the Year. Kimberly Brubaker Bradley and her husband, Bart, have two young children, Matthew and Katie. They live on a farm in eastern Tennessee, in the foothills of the Appalachian Mountains.